Plastic Diamonds

A Novella
by

Susanna Sheehy

Elden Publishing

Elden Publishing, LLC
P.O. Box 421803
Atlanta, GA 30342
susannasheehy@susannasheehy.com

Book cover design by Elden Publishing, LLC
Editing by Arlene Hutchinson

ISBN: 9780978927158
LCCN: 2010925017
Copyright information available upon request

Special thanks to Arlene Hutchinson for editing my book without trying to change the story. You cannot know how valuable that is.

Tuesday

"I can not believe he asked you out." Sylvia rocked herself back in the desk chair of the cubical. She put her feet on Jan's desk and tossed her waist length blond hair over the back of the chair.

"Sylvia, don't do that. If old man Baxter comes by you'll be fired for sure." Sylvia's best friend since kindergarten sat on a stool behind a computer looking bookish. "And I mean it this time, if you mess this job up I'm finished with you. I've been taking care of you for way too long."

"Oh, taking great care of me. I enlist you to help me snag this guy and the next thing I know he's asked you out." Sylvia sat up straight and looked over her shoulder at the sound of footsteps in the hall. "I just don't get it. Why would he ask you and not me? I mean, you know I think you're beautiful but look at you. You dress like a man, wear your hair in a top knot, and I hate to tell you this, Jan, but there are grey streaks in all that black hair you've got piled on your head. You need to find a good colorist."

"I got this suit in women's. It's not a man's suit." Jan looked down at herself. "I even put a pin on the lapel, a daisy. How feminine can you get? Anyway Brent asked me out. So you can just stop putting me down. Obviously, he's interested in more than a pretty face. Of course, I think he just wants to thank me. We've worked on a number of cases together in the last year."

"You're not going are you?"

"Of course I'm not. I wouldn't go out with a man you're hot for." Jan typed something into her computer and picked up the phone to check her messages. "Not that you can say the same thing."

"Oh, that again," Sylvia stood, brushed her hair over her shoulder and straightened her short skirt. "You're never going to let me forget that thing in high school. I mean what could I do? Greg Smable was crazy about me. I don't see how you can blame me when you don't even try to be attractive to men. JanJan, let me take you to my hair dresser. You don't have to be so plain. You know I have gray in my hair, too."

"Now how would anyone know that? You've been a platinum blond since birth. Anyway, with you as my best friend," Jan took a deep breath. "Plain is just going to work better for me."

"I do have nice hair, don't I?" Sylvia smiled and turned to leave the cubicle. She ran smack into the tall broad chest of the subject of their conversation, Brent Barlow. Ohhh, he's gorgeous, she thought as he took her arms to steady her.

"I'm sorry," he said in that deep smooth voice with the slight southern accent. "What is your name again? Sandra?" He smiled and the dimples in his cheeks showed.

"Syl ... Syl ..." She was stuttering. What's wrong with me? I'm not the one that stutters. He's supposed to be stuttering.

"Her name is Sylvia," Jan said smiling faintly. "I'm working on getting this project finished, Brent. I can't talk to you right now." She turned to her computer screen. She had to admit the man was beautiful. His hair was brown and there was gray starting around the temples. It was gorgeous on a man. Not so nice on a woman. She suddenly wished she'd taken Sylvia's advice and gone to a colorist.

"I won't keep you long," he said.

She looked up into his dark brown eyes and felt her mouth fall open. Snapping it shut and catching her tongue between her teeth, she winced and turned back to her computer screen. "I really can't go to the concert with you on Friday, Brent. Thanks for asking. Now Sylvia, please go back to work. I meant what I said about not taking care of you anymore."

Sylvia felt the foolish grin on her face and thought leaving was the best plan. She turned to go, but Brent Barlow detained her with a hand on her arm.

"Wait, don't go yet, Sylvia." He turned to Jan. "I don't care about that concert. If you can't go on Friday, let's do it on Saturday. And Sylvia," he turned back to her and smiled, again stopping her breath in her throat. "Why don't you come along?"

"The three of us?" She swallowed.

"No, we'll make it a foursome. You've met my friend Jeb haven't you Jan?" He looked back.

She could feel laughter trying to force its way to the surface of this conversation. "Yes, he's a nice guy. We had a rousing debate on the wisdom of breeding Staffordshire Terriers."

Sylvia and Brent both looked at her without understanding.

"Pit Bulls,"

"That's right. Jeb has strong opinions about dogs. Actually he has strong opinions about everything." Brent laughed and Sylvia and Jan both smiled stupidly. "Anyway, when he was here the other day he noticed how pretty you are, Sandra."

"Sylvia."

"I'm sorry, Sylvia. I know he'd love to make it a foursome. Come with us." He turned back to Jan. "Please say you'll come."

"Well, I mean, I thought you had a concert on Friday night. Do you have tickets on Saturday, too?" Jan frowned.

"No, I'll find something else to do. You'll have fun. I promise." He looked at Sylvia and tapped her on the elbow. "Talk her into it."

"We'd love to go." Sylvia felt a little agitated. The man was blind. Why couldn't they make it a twosome for crying out loud, him and her?

Brent looked back at Jan and grinned widely. "Good. I'll pick you up at six o'clock."

"That's a long night." Jan said turning back to the computer screen. She really didn't want to do this. She'd never been comfortable with dating.

"It'll fly. You know, time flies when you're having fun." He leaned close to Sylvia and she noticed that his breath smelled like cinnamon. "Thanks," he whispered. "I need all the help I can get." And he left the cube.

"Sylvia, you can't accept a date for me. I really don't want to go. I had plans for Saturday night."

"What were you going to do, wash your hair?"

"Well yes, I always wash my hair on Saturday night. Go back to work. If you don't have a job, you won't be able to support that apartment and I swear you have lived with me for the last time."

"JanJan, I know you love me, even when you act fierce."

Jan took a deep breath and looked back at her friend of thirty years. "Yeah, I don't know what I'd do without you but sometimes I think I'd like to find out."

Sylvia smiled. "I've got to get back to work, JanJan. See you Saturday. I guess I'll come to your place." She stopped. "Don't worry, honey, I'll move in on him during the evening. He'll be putty in my hands, I promise."

"I have no doubt that you're right."

Saturday

Jan Dodd looked at herself in the mirror and took a deep breath. She really didn't want to go out tonight. She'd developed such a nice Saturday routine. Get up early and run around the park, sometimes twice. It was a two and a half mile path right in the heart of Atlanta. It wound around a golf course and was wooded with a tree transplant program. She wasn't sure what that meant but it must be some kind of environmental thing.

Then she would come home and change her clothes and go to her volunteer job at the greyhound rescue shelter. Sometimes Sylvia would join her there. It depended on what she'd done on Friday night.

Not Jan, though. She went home every Friday and ate a vegan meal. She wasn't a vegetarian but Friday was her day of fast. She consumed only fruit and vegetable juice during the day and a meal without meat, fish, dairy products, or eggs after sundown. Those were her rules. Then she would take a long bubble bath and listen to classical music. It was her great indulgence. She'd sleep and wake up to a wonderful day all to herself.

Ruining Saturday with a party on Friday night was out of the question.

Today she'd had to cut her work with the dogs short, though, because instead of watching a movie and eating popcorn at home while doing a deep conditioning treatment on her hair, another indulgence, she had a date with Brent Barlow. How did that happen?

The doorbell to her apartment sounded and she remembered how it had happened. "Sylvia."

"Hey sweetie, I'm sorry I didn't get by the rescue this afternoon." Sylvia breezed into the apartment making it seem way too small like she always did. Sylvia was five feet nine inches of dynamic energy. Jan's own five feet three inches always seemed to shrink next to her and she experienced a brief dip in energy with every encounter. "Some friends and I went dancing last night and I just needed to sleep a little extra. You aren't going out with Brent Barlow looking like that!"

"Brent Barlow asked me to go while I was looking like this." She followed Sylvia into the kitchen. "Why should I change how I look? Obviously he's not interested in me romantically. We just work well together."

"Well, socializing is different than working. Besides," Sylvia cocked her head in perusal. "How are you going to distract Jed while I move in on Brent if you look like a librarian?"

"His name is Jeb." Jan went into the kitchen smoothing the pant suit she'd put on for the evening. "And I'm not a librarian. I'm an account manager for a firm of insurance adjusters."

"A firm of insurance adjusters," Sylvia's voice rose and she rocked her head back and forth sarcastically. "I hate that I do that. It's just so .... so ...."

"It supports you," Jan said. "Do you want some lemonade?"

"Do you have any wine?"

"With you as a best friend, of course I do." Jan pulled a bottle of wine from the refrigerator and poured two glasses.

"You're going to join me, how exciting." Sylvia sipped at her glass. "Now sit down at the table and let me play with your hair."

Jan sipped at her wine and looked at her best friend. She resisted for a minute then sat at the kitchen table. "Syl, please don't make me look stupid. You know how uncomfortable I am with glamour."

"I do know and you're really so beautiful."

Sylvia pulled the pins that held Jan's hair out and let it fall around her shoulders. "I always envied you your curls," she said quietly.

"Shut up, Syl. You never envied me anything." Jan sipped more wine. "And I hate my curls."

"Well, I love them and I have always envied them. I mean not that my platinum blond long thick straight hair won't do but a few curls would be nice." Sylvia laughed as she brushed Jan's hair.

"You know you're the only person who's ever brushed my hair. It feels good." Jan leaned back over the chair and let her best friend pull the brush through her thick curls.

"Didn't your mother brush your hair when you were little?"

"I guess when I was really little she did. All I remember is her insisting that I do it myself because with her and Dad working all the time, I needed to be self-sufficient."

"Poor JanJan, I guess it was good that you had me."

The doorbell rang. "Put it back up." Jan sat up straight and tugged at her hair.

"I will. Calm down." Sylvia pulled the top part up and pinned it loosely. "But only partly. Like I said, you need to be able to distract Jed."

"Jeb,"

"All set?" Brent smiled from the doorway of Jan's apartment.

"I guess so. Would you like to come in? We're drinking a glass of wine." Jan stepped back and Sylvia saw the man standing behind Brent.

"Sure, we'll have a short glass then we're off." Brent entered the apartment and Jan felt the place shrink again. "Jan, you remember my friend Jeb Webb and this is Sandra, Jeb, the accounts payable clerk you thought was so cute."

"Don't describe me as a clerk. It's only what I do for a living." Sylvia stepped forward and extended her hand. "Jeb Webb." She laughed charmingly. "What were your parents thinking?"

"Jebadiah Webb sounded okay. They didn't anticipate the short version of it."

"Oh, well my name is Sylvia. Not Sandra." She edged closer to Brent and looped her arm through his. "Repeat it and maybe you'll remember it." She looked up at him from under her long eyelashes. "Sylvia." Her silky voice purred the name.

"Sylvia." Brent smiled and disengaged his arm. "I'm sorry, I'm terrible with names. Where's the wine." He followed Jan into the kitchen. "That's why I like your name. I can remember it. It's only three letters. J-a-n, it's similar to J-e-b. Good names for my girl and my best friend. I can remember them."

His Girl! Sylvia mouthed to Jan from behind him. Her eyes were wide and her lower lip was definitely leaning toward a pout. Jan shrugged and poured two more glasses of wine.

"I'm not your girl, Brent. I really don't think that's a very funny joke."

"I'm not joking and if you're not my girl now, I'm hoping to win you tonight." He smiled and his dimples showed. "And Jeb's going to win Sylvia, right Jeb? Notice I remembered your name that time." He sat down at the table and Jan took a deep breath and sat down across from him.

Sylvia turned to Jeb and took her first close look at him. He stood about an inch shorter than her. That may have been because of her three inch heels but even in flats he wouldn't be more than a couple of inches taller than her. She liked her men at least six inches taller. His hair was thinning on top and blond but not like hers. It was more the color of soapy water and with that prominent nose who could tell what color his eyes were. The whole package was not unpleasant but certainly nothing to write Mom about. She took the chair next to Brent and Jeb sat down next to Jan.

They make a cute couple, Sylvia thought.

Sylvia and Brent look fantastic together, Jan thought.

"We're going to Medieval Times." Brent sounded excited. "Have you heard of it? They've got huge glasses of beer and they have a show. I even hear the food is good."

"It is good," Sylvia said. "I've been there. It's a blast. When are we supposed to arrive?"

"At seven o'clock. I figured that would give us time if you ran late." Brent smiled at Sylvia. "I know how women like you are?"

"What do you mean women like me?" Sylvia twisted to look at him but he had turned his attention to Jan.

"Then, guess what I've got."

"I can't imagine," Jan said dryly. "Hopefully it isn't contagious."

"Definitely contagious ... doesn't she have a great sense of humor." He smiled across the table to Jeb. "I got late night tickets to the amusement park. We can ride roller coasters and Ferris Wheels. Maybe I can win you a stuffed toy or a gold fish. Don't you think that would win your heart?"

"I don't think I'd better ride a roller coaster after dinner. I don't do too well even on an empty stomach."

"It's an hour from our dinner location. You'll be fine." Brent stood and gulped the last of his wine. "Let's go, the limo is waiting."

"You have a limo?" Jan's heart was beating a little too hard. This whole thing just seemed out of control.

"Don't let him overwhelm you." Jeb put his hand on her arm and she felt her heart slow to normal. She smiled at him. "He has a cab and the driver is a friend of ours. He's giving him a good rate in exchange for babysitting."

"Babysitting?" Jan looked at Brent.

"I like kids," he said. "Let's go."

"I'll sit up front with Ben," Jeb offered when they got to the cab that waited in the parking lot of the apartment complex.

"You know, Brent, we could take my car. You didn't have to hire a cab." Jan wasn't excited about squeezing into the back seat with Brent and Sylvia.

"I'll sit in the middle." Sylvia volunteered.

"No, Jan will sit in the middle. She's such a tiny little thing." Brent smiled down at her. He put his arm on her waist and propelled her toward the open car door. "You get in next to her here, Sandra. I'll go around and get in on the other side."

She stopped and glared at him.

"I was teasing." He laughed. "I know your name is Sylvia." He rounded the car and climbed in next to Jan.

Sylvia slid in beside her on the other side and pinched her leg.

"Ouch." Jan elbowed Sylvia lightly.

"Did I pinch you with my seat belt?" Brent asked concerned as he clicked the belt into place.

"No," she smiled at him. They were eye to eye. The middle seat was higher than the rest and for the first time she noticed the cleft in his square chin. Holy Moly, how many classic features could one person have.

"Here," he reached across her to the shoulder belt in the middle of the bench seat. "I'll help you with your belt. Fasten yours, Sylvia, Jeb, seat belts all around." He pulled the belt across her lightly brushing her small breasts with the back of his hand and fiddling, much too close to her bottom, to snap the belt closed. "All set."

"All set," Jeb said from the front seat.

"I have a car, Jan." Brent continued the conversation. "I just thought a cab would be better, with the giant beer goblets and all. We've already had a glass of wine. Better to have a designated driver, right Ben."

"Right, Brent, and Shannon and I are going to enjoy our two hours alone tomorrow while you take the kids to the amusement park."

"Tonight and tomorrow, too?" Sylvia looked around Jan to Brent.

"It's a different experience with adults than with children. Plus, I got a great deal on the tickets. Don't worry, Ben, I think it'll be a little more than two hours."

"So, Jan," Jeb turned to look back at them from the front seat. "Are you still encouraging the breeding of killer dogs?"

"Staffordshire Terriers are not killer dogs unless someone trains them to be." Jan sat up a little higher.

"You know, darlin," Brent said. "You're always hearing about them killing some child or a neighborhood dog."

"I can assure you that all of those incidents are the fault of the people involved. And don't call me darlin."

"Why not," Brent put his arm across her shoulder and kissed her cheek. "You're absolutely darlin."

"You're making me feel really uncomfortable."

"So how does a dog killing a kid have anything to do with the people?" Jeb diffused the discomfort and Jan blessed him.

"I can assure you that the owners of the dog were remiss and the parents of the child were too. I mean how did the two of them get alone together? Was the dog chained in the yard? Do the owners want aggressiveness from their dog? A lot of times that's why people get those breeds." Jan leaned closer to Sylvia and Brent removed his arm from her shoulder.

"Don't get her talking about dogs," Sylvia said. "She has all sorts of animal causes."

"I didn't notice a dog in your apartment." Brent took her hand and squeezed it. She pulled it away and pushed her hair behind her shoulder.

"Your hair is fine for dinner," Brent said. "But you'll want to pull it back up on top like you usually wear it for the amusement park. Otherwise it'll be flopping all over the place. So why don't you have a dog?"

Jan felt her mouth fall open at his comment about her hair. She also felt Sylvia's mouth fall open and noticed Brent and Jeb looking at both of them.

"I can't afford one right now." Jan snapped her mouth shut and inched closer to Sylvia. "Besides, I'd want to have a greyhound and I need a yard for that."

"I read that those dogs make good apartment dogs. They're couch potatoes." Brent stretched his arm across her shoulder again and pulled her gently toward him.

"They are but they still need to stretch their legs and exercise is good for everyone, whether they want it or not." Jan looked at the ceiling and hoped the ride wasn't too long.

"You should come to the rescue facility sometime, Brent. The dogs are really great. Jan and I work there every Saturday." Sylvia looked around and tried to engage Brent's attention.

"Really," He ignored her and looked straight into Jan's eyes, "Every Saturday."

"I'm there every Saturday." Jan nudged Sylvia with her elbow.

"Oh come on, Jan. I hardly ever miss."

"I'd like to come, Sylvia." Jeb put his hand over the seat and took Sylvia's in his. "I'm really the dog lover. I mean Brent likes dogs but he doesn't fight their causes like I do."

Sylvia looked down to where their hands were joined then up into the dark eyes of Jebediah Webb. She looked a little closer. His eyes seemed to be a very dark blue, almost black. His hand was warm on hers and she felt a sudden flutter in her chest. She cleared her throat. That was not the way this evening was supposed to go.

"Here we are," Brent said as the cab pulled to a stop before a huge castle. He opened his door then turned to unfasten his and Jan's seat belts. In one fluid movement he took her hand and got out of the car pulling her with him.

"It's awfully warm tonight." Jan felt herself being propelled toward the door to the castle. "Are you sure you want to go the amusement park?"

"It'll cool off by midnight," Brent said as he opened the heavy oak doors. "Don't worry about that now. Live for the moment."

"Ahhh, come in honored guests." A man and a woman dressed in medieval clothing greeted them in a large foyer that overlooked a huge arena. Jan's mouth fell open and she turned a circle, stunned by the mere size of the place.

"Fair Lady," the man continued. "I am King Alfonso and this is my lovely daughter, Princess Esperanza. Welcome to our home."

Jan curtseyed then slapped her hand to her mouth. "What did I just do?" she whispered. She could hear Sylvia giggling behind her.

"You curtseyed and quite nicely, I have to say," Brent said quietly in her ear from somewhere behind and above her. "It's so nice to be here, King Alfonso and the fair Princess Esperanza." He took the princess's hand and pretended to kiss it coming about an inch short of contact.

King Alfonso placed a purple crown on Jan's head and Princess Esperanza handed one the same color to Brent. "Please help yourself to our bar before the show then be seated in the purple section for the performance. You'll be cheering for the purple knight throughout the show.

Jan looked back to see Sylvia and Jeb step into the places they had left in front of the King and Princess. Sylvia's curtsey was sweeping and not nearly as silly a bob as she was sure hers was. Of course, Sylvia had a chance to prepare.

"Here we go, Jan," Brent scooped two huge goblets of beer off a table and handed one to her. He showed his tickets to the waitress and she put a mark on both of them. "We get two of these with the tickets but don't worry. If you want more I have cash."

Jan looked at the gigantic blue goblet that she had to hold with two hands. "If I drink this one I won't be able to walk out of here."

"I'll carry you then. Here's our table." He put his beer down then took hers and put it down next to his. He pulled out her chair. "These seats are perfect. Not too close, not too far, a perfect view of the arena."

Jan looked around her. She had to admit the place was getting to her. They had gone back in time. What a strange feeling. She couldn't relate to the costumes and decor.

"You're smiling." Brent tipped up her chin with his hand and she found herself looking into warm brown eyes and a face that looked ... what was the word ... happy. That was it ... completely happy.

She looked at the large glass of beer and resolved not to drink it all. Sylvia stopped at the seat next to her and snapped her small hand bag to the waist of her mini-skirt. Jan looked at her own small shoulder bag and put it over her head and under one arm so it sat more securely in her lap then she sat down.

"Isn't this great, JanJan?" Sylvia beamed from beside her. The purple crown looked brilliant against her shimmering blond hair.

Jan could just imagine how it looked on her black and white striped curls that had surely gone to fuzz in the humidity of the Atlanta summer. "Yeah, it really is."

Jeb sat down on the other side of Sylvia, put one of the King's goblets of beer in front of her and she started to sip. Without thinking Jan took a sip of hers. It was icy cold. Tiny flecks of ice floated in it and the goblet was wet with condensation.

"Thanks for doing this, Brent." Sylvia reached across Jan and put her hand on his wrist. "I love this place and I haven't been here in a while."

He tapped her hand with the finger of his other hand and smiled at her innocently. "Thank Jeb. It was his idea." He turned to put his arm across Jan's shoulders dropping Sylvia's hand to the table. Brushing Jan's cheek lightly with his lips he said, "I had no idea what to do when she turned down my invitation to the concert last night. Thanks Jeb," he leaned around Jan and Sylvia to look at his friend. "This was a great idea."

Just then the master of ceremonies ordered the trumpeters to announce the opening of the ceremonial arena. The crowd all hurried to their assigned areas and found their seats. There was general activity all around and Jan was lost in the excitement. In the arena she watched as the actors and actresses filed in. The knights filed in on horses and stood around the edge of the arena.

"Andalusians," she whispered.

"How did you know?" Brent spoke into her ear.

"I love horses. I've only seen a few of these in real life. Of course, I've studied dozens of pictures of them. Do you suppose we could get close to them?"

"I think we can even get our pictures taken with them. We'll see."

Suddenly there were dozens of servers dressed like wenches and serfs. Their costumes identified them and Jan and Sylvia laughed at the huge amounts of food they delivered, soup in large tureens and roasted meats and vegetables.

"I hate to be a problem, Brent. But I didn't get any silverware," Jan said.

"You don't get silverware, silly," Sylvia nudged her with her elbow. "This is medieval times. There is no silverware."

"You're kidding." Jan looked at Brent as he picked up his soup tureen and sipped.

"No, you're going to eat this meal with your hands." He laughed. "But notice they brought piles of napkins."

While the meal was served and the guests were eating, the legend of the kingdom unfolded in the ceremonial arena. Jan found herself wrapped up completely in the show and was startled when Sylvia tapped her on the arm.

"I'm going to the ladies room," she said. "You must surely have to go. I mean you drank that whole huge goblet of beer."

"I did not." Jan heard her words slur and looked at the empty king's goblet in front of her. "Oh no," she put her hand to her temple. "Do you think I can walk to the ladies room?"

"You'll be fine. I've never seen you eat so much, either."

Jan looked down at her plate. It was littered with chicken bones, rib bones, potato skins. Chunks of bread swam in gravy and salad leaves spilled onto the table. "Look at the mess I made."

"Like a true medieval princess." Brent smiled.

"I'm going to the ladies room with Sylvia."

"Good, I'll go now, too. I think the sparring is over." Brent got up and walked with them toward to the restrooms.

"I'll get us another round," Jeb called after them. "We'll all be back just in time for the jousting."

"Great, he's getting us another round. Sylvia, you know I'm already past my limit," Jan said from the stall next to Sylvia's. She was amazed at the length of the flow. "I've never peed that much in my life," she said as she flushed the toilet.

"You've never drunk a whole King's goblet of beer before either." Sylvia put on her lipstick then blotted it with a paper towel. "You'll be alright, you ate really well. Just don't drink the second round."

"I wasn't planning to drink the first round but the next thing I knew it was gone. Are you sure you didn't drink it."

"Why would you have peed that much if I drank it?"

"That's true."

"Now, here's what I want you to do," Sylvia said. "Change places with Brent."

"How am I supposed to get him to change places with me?" Jan washed her hands then scrubbed a smudge off her chin.

"Tell him you can't see."

"The show's half over. He knows I can see."

"Tell him there's something wrong with your chair."

"If he sits in it he'll know I was lying. I don't know how I let you get me into this mess, Sylvia." Jan looked in the mirror and laughed. Her cheeks were pink and her eyes were overly bright. The purple crown, just as she had suspected, looked ridiculous on her black hair. The white streaks reflected in the shiny material and the curls and frizz were trying to overtake the crown like weeds on a garden wall. "I want to go home."

"Well, you can't for a while. We're going to the amusement park, remember? Of course, that will surely take care of him ever wanting to go out with you again. I can't wait to see the look on his face when you puke on the first roller coaster."

"Sylvia, please help me." Jan wiped her hands on a towel and looked up at her friend.

"I will, sweetie, just change seats with Brent."

Jan sat down at the table next to Brent and rubbed her neck. She rotated her head a few times then laid her forehead on the table.

"JanJan," Sylvia put her hand on Jan's neck. "You okay, what's wrong?"

"My neck is stiff again."

"Oh, no," Sylvia looked at Brent and swallowed. The look of concern on his face was so intense. "She has a bad disk or something," she said.

"That's right. Sometimes when I look in the same direction for too long my neck gets stiff."

"Why don't you and I switch places with Sylvia and Jeb? They could move to this end and we could go down there," Brent suggested.

"No," Sylvia still wouldn't be sitting next to Brent. "Why don't you just switch places with me, Brent? Then the angle would be just enough different to relieve it."

"Sure, darlin, I want you to be comfortable." Brent stood and helped Jan move to his seat while he edged in between her and Sylvia.

"This is better anyway," Sylvia looped her arm through his, "boy, girl, boy, girl."

"I guess so." Brent looked over at Jeb. "Thanks for the beers, Jeb. Be sure to save the tickets. We don't get any more drinks but the tickets get us into the Knight's club for dancing and pictures. Jan wants her picture taken with one of the horses, don't you darlin." He turned back to her and frowned. "Does your neck hurt? Here let me rub it." He raised both hands to Jan's neck once again dropping Sylvia's arm to the table.

"Hey," she said. Brent didn't hear her.

Jeb chuckled from beside her and she gave him a withering look. "Ouch ..." He grabbed his chest and laughed again. Sylvia reluctantly laughed with him.

In the arena the six knights of different colors competed in contest after contest of skill. They were throwing flags and javelins and tossing rings. When the last contest was over, the squires, whose costumes were labeled, came out and prepared the arena for jousting.

"What's jousting?" Jan asked turning to stop Brent from massaging her shoulders. She'd forgotten she objected. It felt so good.

"The knights fight with swords and lances for the fair maiden's hand."

"You're kidding." Jan knit her brows. "Isn't that dangerous? I mean the men are wearing armor but what about the horses."

"It's pretend, darlin. Don't worry."

The jousting began and the sound of metal clashing woke the whole crowd. The cheering from the different colored sections was deafening. The Knights first fought to unhorse each other but once on the ground they continued until only one was left to claim the championship and the fair maiden. At the end the crowd roared and Jan jumped up in excitement, knocking her Kings goblet over toward her. She jumped back to avoid the spill only to find it was empty. She'd drunk the whole thing again. She looked down at her plate to find a pile of dirty napkins and crumbs and smears of pastries and pies.

"I need to go to the bathroom again."

"I'll come with you." Sylvia stood and took her arm and they wound through the crowd.

"That was a great trick about the stiff neck, Jan. Worked like a charm," Sylvia said from the stall next to hers. "Unfortunately, I spent the last part of the show looking at Brent's back while he rubbed your neck."

"Wow, what a flow. You know, Syl, it feels good to pee like that."

"JanJan, I told you not to drink that second goblet. There are probably at least twenty four ounces in each one of those." She was standing at the mirror when Jan left the stall. Her lipstick was already in place. "Maybe, I should try to talk Brent into calling it a night. I'm not getting anywhere with him and I'm getting worried about you."

"Don't worry about me, Syl. I'm having a really good time." She looked in the mirror and attempted to smooth her hair, grinned at the failed attempt and took a tube of lip balm out of the purse that hung at her waist.

"What else do you have in that purse?"

"My driver's license and my credit card," Jan looked inside the small bag. "Five dollars and some mints."

"The bare essentials," Sylvia laughed. "You're something else, JanJan. Let's go talk those guys into taking us home."

"Well, we don't have to go to the amusement park but I want my picture taken with one of those Andalusian horses."

"Okay, okay, I guess I wouldn't mind posing for some pictures, too."

Jan walked into the Knight's club on Brent's arm feeling like a princess. She felt a nagging sense of having forgotten something, like maybe why she was there. She'd certainly never done anything like this before. Brent led her straight to the dance floor and took her in his arms. She'd been afraid that the buzzy feeling she'd attributed to the beer she'd drunk would turn into the spins when she started to dance but it didn't. Brent held her by the waist and the hand and she seemed to be able to float in his arms.

"I thought a little exercise would do us good before we try to drink anything else." His low husky voice sounded in her ear.

"I don't think I'll try to drink anything else." She looked up at him and their lips were almost touching. He smelled like beer and smoke from the fireplaces and Jan wished he would kiss her right there on the dance floor.

"That's probably a good idea if we're going to ride roller coasters afterward. I'll get us a glass of water in a minute and we can go and find those horses."

"Silly me," Jan looked back down. She'd thought he was going to kiss her. She'd hoped he was going to kiss her.

"Why do you say you're silly?"

"No reason."

"I think I'll just sit for a minute before we have our pictures taken," Sylvia said to Jeb and she made herself comfortable at one of the tables around the dance floor.

"Sylvia, please dance with me?"

She looked up into his face. He was smiling and holding out his hand. His eyes were hidden again behind his prominent nose but she noticed for the first time that his nose, though large, was straight and very attractive. He reached down and took her hand from where it lay on the table.

"It's not often that I get to have the most beautiful woman in the kingdom as my date," he said as he pulled her to her feet and onto the dance floor.

"The most beautiful woman in the kingdom," she laughed. "I'm feeling invisible tonight."

"I've noticed you and you've been on my arm all night. I may never wash my arm again." He put his hand on her waist and guided her into a dance.

"I don't think they danced this close in medieval times."

"Hey, it's the twenty-first century."

She put her hand on his shoulder and let him lead her around the dance floor. "Doesn't it bother you that I'm taller than you are?" Sylvia asked after a few minutes.

"I don't actually think you're taller than me. I think your shoes are taller than me." They both laughed. "But no, even if you were taller than me in your stocking feet I'd still feel ten feet tall because I'm dancing with the most beautiful woman in the kingdom."

Sylvia looked at him, their lips were almost touching. Would he kiss her? Should she kiss him?

"Hey guys," Brent said from behind Sylvia. The knights and horses are in the arena for pictures. Come on."

Sylvia released a breath she didn't know she was holding and turned to follow Brent and Jan to the arena.

"Look, Syl. They have props." Jan was on a dappled gray horse wearing a cape that draped over the back of the horse and hung to the ground. The handler made the horse bow down on one knee. Brent stood at the head of the horse with a shield and a sword. The photographer snapped the picture. Sylvia laughed and sipped her sparkling water while she and Jeb watched Brent and Jan pose for a number of different pictures. The lights were spectacular and the pictures were digital so they got a CD to take home when they were finished.

"Well," Brent said. "I guess we'd better go if we're going to the amusement park. "It's ten o'clock."

"Wait," Jeb said. "Sylvia and I need pictures." He took the cape from Jan's shoulders and draped it over his own. He climbed up on the horse and allowed the handler to put the animal in a bow.

Sylvia laughed, took the sword and shield from Brent and stood at the head of the horse.

"I'm just not sure it's a good idea, Brent," Sylvia said. They were once again in the back of the cab with Jan in the middle. Sylvia had noticed the studious look Jan had as she stared straight ahead at the highway traffic in front of them. "Jan gets car sick riding in a car at night. I can tell she's concentrating on not puking right now."

"Is that true, darlin?" Brent took Jan's hand.

"Don't distract me." She shook his hand off and gripped her knees.

"Pull over, Ben." Brent tapped the driver on the shoulder. "Jeb, you switch places with Jan. If she rides up front she won't get sick. Why didn't you tell me?" he said as he helped her out of the car and walked her around to the passenger seat. "I would have understood."

Sylvia smiled as she scooted into the middle seat. Good work on her part and Jan's. Now he really couldn't turn his back on her. Jeb slipped into the door on the other side and Brent returned to his seat. She looked from one of them to the other. Things were looking up in this evening. If only it didn't take too much of a toll on Jan.

"Do you feel better up there, sweetie?" she asked Jan.

"A little bit."

She took a deep breath. It was time for truth, even if she was sitting between two men, one of them the most gorgeous creature in the world and one of them the nicest. "Brent, Jeb, I think you need to know that Jan vomits on amusement park rides."

"That's not true, Sylvia," Jan objected turning around to glare at her then whirling back to watch the road trying obviously to control her gag reflex. "I've ... never ... vomited ... on ... a ride. In a car is a different matter."

"Jan, remember when we were kids and all the parents in the school purchased season tickets to the park? You always stayed at the bottom and held everyone's purses and packages, remember?"

"Yes,"

"Why did you do that?"

"I was afraid I would vomit on the ride."

"You never even tried?" Sylvia sat forward and Brent and Jeb both took an arm and pulled her back. "I mean, you think you know someone. I thought you had a weak stomach. I didn't know you were a coward."

"Hey, watch what you say about Jan," Brent said.

The car pulled to a stop in front of the gate. "I do have a weak stomach. In fact it's a good damn thing this car stopped because I was just about to lose control." Jan jumped out of the car and clutching her stomach started to pace back and forth in front of the gate.

"So," Sylvia looked from Brent to Jeb. "Do you still want to go in there?"

"Yes," Brent handed out the tickets. "If you don't, I'll let Ben take you home and come back for us. Okay with you, Ben?"

"You're picking the kids up at two tomorrow, right?"

"You bet, right after church."

"No," Sylvia said. "I guess if she's staying, I'd better. Someone needs to pick up the pieces."

"I'm really wondering about your intelligence, Brent," Sylvia said sipping on a glass of wine at the tavern. "I didn't know this park opened a tavern for adults at night."

"A small amount of wine is just the thing for her. Go ahead, darlin, drink it," he said. "If I'd known she was such a light weight, I wouldn't have gotten that second round."

"I'm not a light weight." Jan picked up the glass and sipped. "And you know what, I'm feeling better already. I'm ready for one of those roller coasters."

"Okay, but I'm not sitting behind you." Sylvia got up and followed the crowd to the first ride.

Jan let Sylvia and Jeb get into the seat in front then she and Brent got in and pulled the bar back over both of them. She felt it snap into place and then the cars lurched forward and started to chug up the track. She held her breath all the way to the top of the first hill. "Oh no!" she said. Then they were plunging downward so steep and so fast she couldn't see the tracks.

Someone was screaming and someone was laughing or maybe that was the same voice doing both. She looked around. Everyone was screaming and everyone was laughing. She looked forward to where Sylvia and Jeb were holding their hands in the air, the center ones joined. She looked next to her where Brent watched her laughing and screaming. Their hands were clamped to the bar, the center ones joined.

The coaster rolled into the station and Brent helped her out of the seat. She looked up at his smiling face then at Sylvia and Jeb. They were all looking at her anxious but smiling.

"I didn't throw up," she screamed and laughed. "That was a blast. Can we go again?" Brent picked her up and swung her around then Sylvia did the same and Jeb put a hand on her shoulder.

"There are six roller coasters in this place. Let's ride the others then if you want to start over we'll do it," Jeb said. "What about a coke or something?"

"No I just want to go on another ride."

"Alright, we've ridden every roller coaster in the place. I won you a teddy bear, a gold fish, and a diamond ring. Have I won the fair maiden's heart yet?" Brent asked. They were sitting on a bench watching Jeb try to hit a gong to win a prize for Sylvia and not managing to do it.

Jan looked at the huge plastic diamond she had on her middle finger and smiled. "I've had a wonderful time, Brent. I don't know why you did this for me but I enjoyed it."

"Good," he smiled and stood as Jeb and Sylvia approached. "Let's ride the Ferris wheel. It's so quiet and romantic. Just one more ride, okay, Jan. Then I'll take you home."

Jan looked at the Ferris wheel. It moved slowly around in a circle going high in the sky and nearly brushing the ground. There was music playing and the night was still warm. High in the air like that it was probably much cooler. It did look romantic. She felt her heart flutter and she warmed at the thought of snuggling up to Brent. Uh oh, she really wanted to snuggle up to Brent.

"I'll bet its cooler up there," Brent said and she blushed at her thoughts.

"I'd like to ride it," Sylvia said. "You can wait down here if you want, JanJan."

"No, I'd like to go." They walked over to the ride and got into the line.

Brent handed her in and got in after her snuggling close. Sylvia and Jeb had gotten on before them and the ride started. It was wonderful. The seat rocked gently as the huge wheel rose high into the sky. The air was cooler and there was a small night breeze. The music was soothing. Up they went all the way to the top and over the edge to slowly descend. Brent put his arm around her and pulled her close. Jan closed her eyes as they started their second ascent. She opened them just as they got to the top and started back down.

"Uh oh," she whispered as her head began to swim.

"Jan, darlin, what's wrong?" Brent squeezed her shoulder.

She pulled away from him and clamped her hand over her mouth as her stomach lurched.

"Lean over the side."

"No, I'll throw up on Sylvia and Jeb." She looked around frantically as she felt her control slipping. Then she noticed the small purse hanging in her lap. She pulled it open just in time and wretched violently into it. "I'm sorry," she whimpered and dissolved into tears.

"Sweetie, just pitch the purse," Sylvia said as she bathed Jan's face in the bathroom sink.

"No, I have to get my credit card and license out. I'll let the five dollars and the mints and lip balm go." She reached inside and extracted the dripping cards, slapped them on the counter and ran into the bathroom stall to heave a little harder. "I wish I could just crawl into the toilet and let you flush me down," she said appearing white faced a minute later.

"Well you can't so come over here and let me clean you up," Sylvia said. "First, we'll just fill this sink with soapy water and you can knock the defiled cards into it."

Jan did as she was told and Sylvia said, "There you go. Now wash your hands. Okay, here I'll dry the cards."

Jan felt completely limp. "What time is it anyway?"

"It's twelve thirty."

"I have to go to Mass in less than twelve hours." Jan rinsed her mouth and spat. I wish I had my mints."

"Here, I have some." Sylvia reached into the purse she had clipped to her belt and handed a mint to Jan. "You know you could go to the five thirty pm service. Besides you'll feel fine tomorrow. Throwing up always makes the hangover better."

"I just want to go home." Jan buried her face in Sylvia's shirt and cried.

Sylvia held her and cooed softly to her as she guided her out of the public bathroom at the amusement park.

"I'm glad you came out," Jeb said. "I'm not sure how much longer I could have kept him from going in after you." He gestured to Brent who was prying Jan away from Sylvia's shoulder.

"I'm so sorry, darlin." Brent spoke gently to her. "I'm overwhelming some times. Jeb told me I was overdoing it but I just didn't listen. Where's her purse?" He asked Sylvia.

"We saved her driver's license and credit card. I've got them in my pouch but we sacrificed the purse."

"I'll get you a new purse. I promise." He guided her to the gate of the park where Ben was waiting.

"I just want to go home," Jan said. She was vaguely aware of saying it several times.

Sunday

Jan stretched her leg out under the covers of her bed and made contact with someone else's leg. She jerked her foot away and opened one eye.

"Hey," Sylvia laughed. "Don't worry it's just me. Don't tell me you don't remember coming home last night. You didn't drink that much."

"I don't drink, Syl. It was a lot for me." She rolled over and sat up slowly swinging her legs over the side of the bed. "I don't feel too bad, though," she said touching her temple. "I've got a little headache but that may be because my neck is stiff from all those roller coaster rides."

"I told you puking prevents a hangover." Sylvia slid out from under the covers and went into the bathroom. "You have to admit you had fun last night."

"There's a new toothbrush in the second drawer." Jan called.

"I know." Sylvia appeared at the door with a lathered toothbrush in her mouth.

"Thanks for staying Sylvia." Jan looked at the clock. "Good, it's only nine o'clock. I have time to go for a walk before church." She went to the kitchen to put on a pot of coffee.

"I was thinking," Sylvia came into the kitchen dressed in the clothes she had worn the night before. "I'm going to my parents' farm in Danielsville today. My sister and her kids are coming from Charlotte and I haven't seen the new baby. My brothers will both be there with their families. Why don't you come with me? It would be nice to have the company on the drive and they go to mass at five thirty. We could go with them, then have dinner and drive back afterward."

"We wouldn't get home until ten o'clock at least. We have to work tomorrow. Besides I get car sick at night."

"I'll let you drive back. You don't get car sick when you drive and it's only an hour away. We might get home by nine and besides, ten isn't too late. What time do you go to bed on a work night anyway?"

"Nine, but I usually read." She sounded defensive even to herself. "I don't think so today, Sylvia, but thanks for inviting me. I'd love to see your family but I think I need a quiet day to recover from last night."

"That's what worries me." Sylvia sipped the coffee that Jan poured for her. "You'll sit around here all day and stew about your behavior last night and you were fine. We had fun. I know I did, even if Brent didn't pay any attention to me."

"Yeah, what happened to putty in your hands? Do you want some toast?" She asked as she pulled the bread out of the refrigerator.

"No thanks, I can't stand that healthy stuff you buy. I don't know what happened with Brent but I'm not giving up. Next time I'll distract him."

"There isn't going to be a next time." Jan pushed the lever on the toaster. "You're on your own."

"If he asks you there will be a next time. You have to say yes." Sylvia stood and snapped her purse to her belt and picked up her car keys. "Of course you have to find a way to include me. If he doesn't ask you out again then I'm on my own and that's fine. I work better on my own anyway."

"Why would he ask me out again, Syl? I threw up in my purse."

Sylvia smiled. "Yeah, that was great. At least you know it's not roller coasters that make you sick. You just have to stay away from Ferris Wheels. Knowing you, I wouldn't recommend Merry-Go-Rounds either." She chuckled.

"Oh, I'm so humiliated." Jan covered her face with her hands.

"See what I mean. You shouldn't be alone all day, honey. Come with me."

"No thanks, not today. Don't worry about me. I'll distract myself with a good book."

The phone was ringing when Jan got out of the shower but she ignored it. She toweled off and put on her running clothes. She would shower again after her run but she felt grimy from the activities of the night before, even though she vaguely remembered Sylvia putting her in the shower when they got home last night.

"I'll put on extra moisturizing cream," she said to herself as she got ready to go to the park for a run. She had planned a walk but today she knew it would turn into a run. She looked at the answering machine and saw the flashing red light. She pressed the button.

"Good Mornin, darlin," it was Brent's deep voice. "I'll call back, but let me tell you now. I'm picking the kids up at two o'clock and I should be at your house at two thirty. I hope you'll go back to the amusement park with me today. Don't worry. We'll stay away from the Ferris Wheel."

"I didn't agree to go with him today," she said out loud again. "Have I always talked to myself?"

The phone rang just as she was closing the door to her apartment. "Should I get that?"

"I would," her neighbor said from behind her. "It might be important."

"Good Morning, Mr. Sams." She opened her door and ran back into the apartment. "Hello?"

"Jan, this is Brent."

"You just called." That was a stupid thing to say. "I got your message. I can't go today. Thanks anyway."

"Please,"

Jan took a deep breath. Why is he so persistent? "I have plans."

"Change them."

"I can't. I mean what about Sylvia?"

The line was quiet then Brent said, "I only have one extra ticket. But if your plans are with her that's fine, we'll buy a ticket at the gate. Jeb can't come today, though, he's visiting his family."

"Don't tell me they live in Danielsville."

There was another pause on the line. "No, they live here, why?"

"No reason. Let me see if I can get in touch with Sylvia but, Brent, I really don't think we can go today."

"Listen, I'm going to come by your apartment at two thirty. I know I'm gambling but I'm hoping I can talk you into going. You'll love Ben's kids and like I said last night, the amusement park is a whole different experience with children. See ya."

Jan listened to the dial tone for a minute before she hung up the phone. "I wish I hadn't answered that."

Well she just wouldn't be there at two thirty. Jan was jogging on the path at the park. It was late August in Atlanta and the mornings were cooler now than they'd been in July. Not much cooler but a little. She felt guilty. There was no way to include Sylvia today. She had tried to call her on her cell phone but when she reached her the phone went dead before she could tell her about Brent. She probably wouldn't have come back anyway. Sylvia was very close to her family and Jan knew she couldn't wait to meet her new nephew.

No, Sylvia would have just told her to say no. Didn't she realize how hard it was to say no to Brent Barlow?

"Jan." She heard Jeb Webb's voice from behind her. She tried to pretend she hadn't heard it but he called her again and she had to turn around. "I thought you were visiting your family today," she said.

He looked puzzled as he ran toward her. "How did you know that?"

"Brent told me." She started to jog beside him down the trail.

"That's right. He was going to ask you to go with him and the kids today. I'll visit my family this afternoon. Are you going to the amusement park?"

"No, Sylvia's gone to Danielsville to see her family and there's no reason for me to go without her."

"She's got a thing for Brent, doesn't she?"

"Yeah,"

"And you're trying to help her bring him around."

"Well, I guess that's what I was doing last night but it won't happen today if she can't even be there."

"You know Brent didn't invite her to go to the amusement park with him. He invited you."

"I know. He's just being nice because we work together. He and Sylvia make a beautiful couple. Didn't you notice that last night?" She felt sad for some reason.

"Yeah, but Brent doesn't even know what she looks like. He doesn't even care. Truth is he doesn't even know what he looks like." Jeb laughed. "And he doesn't even care."

"Oh come on, everyone knows what they look like and everyone knows Sylvia is beautiful," she said. "Everyone knows Brent is handsome, too."

"Well, I suppose he can recognize himself in a mirror and on some level he knows Sylvia is beautiful but like I said. He doesn't care." They jogged in silence for a minute. "Brent just doesn't care about that kind of thing."

"Well, when he gets to know Sylvia he'll love her. She's not just a pretty face you know."

"I know she's not. In fact, she's very smart and talented, too. She's got a good heart and she's a lot of fun."

Jan looked sideways at Jeb. He was a nice looking man. His hairline may be receding but his eyes were intense and a very dark blue. His nose was a little big but it wasn't ugly. In fact it was distinguished looking. She wondered if Sylvia had noticed any of that when she was out with him last night.

"You have a crush on her, don't you?" She sighed at his affirming silence. "I'm sorry, Jeb. She's got her sights set on Brent. You don't stand a chance. How do you know she's talented?"

"I went by her desk the other day. I was going to ask her to lunch and I saw that calendar she has in the mat on her desk. She's drawn all sorts of beautiful pictures in the spaces."

"She's not supposed to be drawing pictures." Jan bristled. "She's supposed to be working."

"Maybe she should be working at drawing pictures. Jan, I hate to tell you this, but Sylvia doesn't stand a chance with Brent either. If Brent hasn't noticed her by now, he isn't going to. He and Ben and I have been best buddies since kindergarten. I know him."

"Really, Sylvia and I have been friends since kindergarten, too."

"So you're the same age." He paused, thoughtfully.

"Yes, you sound surprised."

"No." Jeb changed the subject. "Honestly, when we were teens Ben and I wondered if Brent was gay. With his looks all the girls in the school were after him and he was oblivious. Then when we were in our twenties we figured since he never paid attention to men either, that he must just have no interest in romance." They slowed to a walk as they started toward the entrance of the park. "You know, Jan, he's paid more attention to you than he ever has to any woman. If he's interested in anyone, it's you."

"I'm sure that's not true," Jan said. "Not with Sylvia in the picture. Besides, I'm just a plain Jane. Actually, I'm not even that, I'm a plain Jan." She laughed. "Here's my car. It was nice running with you, Jeb. Do you run here often?"

"Yeah, I like this park. The trail is nice and it's not far from where I live. I'm going around again." He started down the trail. "Have fun at the amusement park."

"I'm not going to the amusement park," she said but he'd gone around a curve in the trail and was out of sight.

He couldn't be interested in me. Jan thought as she let herself into her apartment after church. What a stupid thought. He was very attentive last night but I think he just likes me. I mean we've worked together for over a year.

He was on the interview team when she applied for her job a year ago. They had been in meetings together and worked on several accounts together. They had a good professional relationship.

She went into the bathroom and looked into the mirror. Absolutely not, there was no way Brent Barlow was attracted to her when Sylvia was on the scene. Her skin was so white you could see pink veins beneath it and it tended to flame every time anyone talked to her. If she had to say anything in a meeting her nose glowed red. She could lead a sleigh through the fog.

Her hair was a mass of dark curls and in the humid Georgia summer it frizzed all over the place. She didn't even want to think about how much money she spent on mousse to keep it smoothed into a knot at the top of her head. Her eyes weren't blue and they weren't gray. They were somewhere in between with yellow specks in them. Now that was just weird. Nobody has yellow eyes. She shrugged and moved away from the mirror.

No reason to worry. For a minute she'd worried that she was moving in on Sylvia's boyfriend but that was not going to be a problem. She laughed at the thought. The doorbell rang and she went to see who it was.

"It's only one-thirty," she said as she opened the door to none other than Brent Barlow.

"I was afraid if I came at two-thirty you would try to avoid me by not being here."

"Why would I do that?" She hoped her face wasn't turning red. She had planned to do exactly that.

"I'm not sure but I was worried about it so I figured I'd catch you now and you can go with me to pick the kids up. Come on, Jan. I promise you'll have fun. Change your clothes. You'll be more comfortable in jeans and a T-shirt. Mel and Jack love the water rides, so we'll spend most of our time wet."

Water rides and a t-shirt, Jan thought, did he want to get a look at her breasts? She looked down at her meager endowment and shrugged. No problem there. "Brent, I threw up on a Ferris Wheel. I really don't want to try a water ride."

"They're more like the roller coasters. I don't think you'll have a problem but if you don't want to go you can stay at the bottom and hold the bags. Kids love to buy stuff and Uncle Brent's a pushover. There will be a lot of bags. Now go change your clothes. We have to pick up Mel and Jack in twenty minutes."

Jan went into her bedroom and shut the door. Why didn't she just say no? Well, she had said no and he had overruled her. She pulled on a pair of blue jeans and a t-shirt then thought better of it and put on a cotton blouse. She put on her sneakers and went back into the living room.

"I called Ben and told him we'd be a little late. He was miffed." Brent smiled and the dimples in his cheeks flashed. "He can't wait for time alone with Shannon. You'll love Shannon. She's a great girl and treats my friend Ben like a king. Come on, let's go."

Jan locked the door as they went out and wondered again how she'd gotten talked into doing this.

"Uncle Brent!" A blond headed girl about ten years old launched herself at Brent as the front door to the house opened. "I didn't think you'd ever get here."

Brent picked her up and spun her around. "Well I'm here. I want you to meet my friend Jan," he said as he put her down. "Jan this is Melanie. I call her Mel. Jack come over here and meet Jan."

A boy of about six walked over to the front door looking shy. He shook Jan's hand and said to Brent. "I was hoping you'd bring Uncle Jeb."

Jan pulled her hand away and cleared her throat. "Don't worry, Jack, I wanted him to bring Uncle Jeb, too."

The boy looked up at her and smiled. "You don't want to go either?"

"Not much," she said. "Why don't you want to go?"

"I don't like those river rides and Uncle Brent and Mel won't do much else."

"I've never been on a river ride," Jan said. "Why don't you like them?"

"I can't swim. Mel's on a swim team."

"Do you have to swim?"

"No," Jack said. "But there's a lot of water."

Ben came into the foyer with a small pretty woman with wavy red hair. "Hey, Brent, hello, Jan," he said, "Jan, this is Shannon, my wife."

"Jack, you're not upsetting Jan are you?" Shannon said. "He's not as excited about the amusement park as Brent and Melanie are. He likes to go with Jeb because they'll split up and do the things he likes to do."

"I'm not so sure about the water rides, myself," Jan said. "I suppose Ben told you what happened to me last night."

"No," Shannon looked at her husband. "What happened?"

"I'll let Jan tell you someday," Ben said as he handed Jack his backpack. "No need to put this on now but it'll come in handy at the park. Be good guys." He handed Melanie a similar bag and hurried them out the door. Jan found herself in the front seat of Brent's car with two kids in the back.

"I didn't know you were afraid of the water rides, Jack," Brent said as they stood in line to get into the park.

"Aww, the poor baby," Melanie teased.

"I'm not afraid. I just don't like them."

"What do you like to do, Jack?" Jan asked.

"I like the arcade and I like the mine car."

"That's the baby roller coaster."

"Melanie," Jan said. "How old are you?"

"I'm ten years old."

"How old are you, Jack?"

"I'm six."

"He is not," Melanie said. "He won't be six until next month. He isn't even old enough for first grade. He's in kindergarten."

"I wonder how you would have felt about a water ride when you were six," Jan said.

"Actually, Jan," Brent smiled at her. "She loved them."

"Shut up, Brent."

"Why are you smiling?" Jan looked at Brent as they stood in line for the first water ride.

"Shut up Brent, is the most intimate thing you've ever said to me."

She looked sharply at him. Why did he want her to say anything intimate? "Shut up."

He widened his smile and she noticed for the first time that his teeth were perfectly straight and very white. "You said it again."

"So why are we going on a water ride when Jack and I don't want to. That's half the people," Jan said. "Why don't you and Melanie do what you want to and we'll do what we want to?"

"Because we have to stay together," Brent said. "I didn't bring you so we could separate."

"Well, I don't want to go on this ride."

"Don't fight it, Jan." Jack tugged on her hand. "I'll help you."

She looked down at the little boy. He stood a little straighter and he held his chin higher. "Jack, I hate to tell you this but I threw up on the Ferris Wheel last night."

"I threw up on the Ferris Wheel too one time. They don't make me ride it any more. I wish I'd throw up on the water rides but I don't." Jack squeezed her hand. "I'll help you. Let's just ride this one then we can go to the mine car."

"I can't believe you're forcing this child to go on a ride that scares him," she said to Brent.

Brent looked at her and then at Jack. "I'm sorry. I'm being overwhelming again, aren't I? You guys don't have to go."

"The babies," Melanie said.

"Melanie, that's not nice." He looked back at Jack.

"I'm going," the boy said. "You can stay here if you want, Jan."

She looked at the child clinging to her hand. "No, I'll go too, but I want to sit next to Jack." She leaned down to speak into his ear. "Maybe I'll throw up. Then we can ride whatever we want to."

Jack smiled and they stepped onto the raft and buckled their seat belts.

"I need to sit down," Jan said as she came off the ride. She went straight to a bench and sat checking the purse she had fastened to the waist of her jeans.

"It wasn't too bad, was it?" Jack followed her and stood in front of her.

"Thanks to you ..." She looked at the child. Her stomach had started to churn when the raft had first started to float away from the dock. Then the small soft hand had reached out to clutch hers and she felt grounded.

"Thanks Jack. Sorry I didn't throw up but, you know what, I almost enjoyed it."

"Me, too," he said. "Can we go to the mine car now?" They both looked up at Brent and Melanie.

"Sure," Brent said.

"Uncle Brent, that's a baby ride."

Brent looked at Melanie as if seeing her for the first time. "No it isn't. In fact, I love that ride. You can wait at the bottom and hold the packages if you want."

"We don't have any packages yet," she said, pouting. She looked up at Brent, studied his face for a minute then said, "Alright, we'll go on the mine car."

"Ben says we can take the kid's to dinner as long as we're home by eight." He smiled as he hung up his cell phone. "He sounded sleepy. I'll bet you he and Shannon have spent the whole afternoon in bed."

Jan looked away from the gleam in his eye. "I'll probably be alright then. It doesn't get completely dark by eight."

Brent looked at her puzzled. "Oh that's right, you get car sick at night. Does it help if you drive?"

"Yes, but I'm not going to drive your car. It's a Jaguar. I drive a Ford."

"Same thing," he guided her to the driver's seat of his car and handed her the keys. "Where do you want to go, guys?"

"Chuck E. Cheese!" They chimed in unison.

"What is Chunky Cheese?" Jan asked as she turned the key in the ignition.

"Chuck E. Cheese," Brent laughed. "Can't describe it, I'll tell you how to get there."

"That was fun, Brent," Jan said when he walked her to her door. It was nine o'clock, her bedtime. They had dropped the tired kids off at eight and Ben and Shannon, looking happy and refreshed, had insisted that they stay for a glass of wine. The kids were sent to their bedrooms to settle down and Brent and Jan had chatted happily about the day.

"You're not going to ask me in?" Brent asked as she put her key in the lock.

"It's my bedtime. I like to read and go to bed early on Sunday night. It gives me a good start to the week." She smiled up at him.

"And you always start the week with a smile. Thanks for coming with me today. You created a whole different experience for Jack. I figured you would." He looked down at her and she melted from the warmth of his smile. Then he kissed her, taking her completely by surprise. His lips were warm and firm on hers and the bristles of his beard brushed her chin. She felt dazed as she looked up at him when he pulled away. "See you tomorrow, now go inside so I can be sure you're safe." He opened the door and propelled her through it.

She locked the door behind her and went into her bedroom.

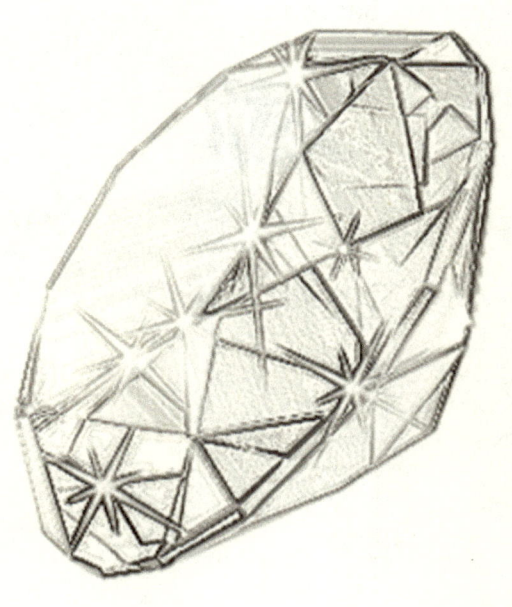

Monday

"You're not going to believe how adorable little Punjab is." Sylvia sat down on the rolling stool in Jan's cubicle at the firm.

"Punjab?" Jan turned from her computer and blinked at her friend. "They named him Punjab?"

"Well, not forever. None of the names they had picked out for him fit and they had to fill out a birth certificate so that's what they put. They'll change it as soon as they come up with something else. But like I said, he's adorable. He looks just like me."

"He looks just like Barbara, you mean." Jan turned back to her computer.

"Same thing, we're sisters. So I hope you didn't pine away yesterday about throwing up on Saturday night."

Jan stiffened and concentrated harder on the screen of her computer.

"Well, Jan," Sylvia persisted. "Tell me you're alright. I worried all day."

"What time did you get home?"

"Ten-thirty,"

"See I told you it would be past my bedtime." Jan typed something on the keyboard.

"Jan, you were alright yesterday weren't you?"

"Actually," she turned and looked at Sylvia. "I ended up going back to the amusement park with Brent and Ben's kids."

Sylvia sat up a little straighter and looked her in the eye.

"Jeb couldn't go because he was visiting his family, so Brent asked me to go. I tried to call you, remember your cell phone was out of range." She was babbling. Why? She had nothing to feel guilty about, except the kiss and that was innocent. Jan looked at her beautiful friend and remembered her own reflection in the mirror. She relaxed. It was ridiculous to even think Brent was interested in her and not Sylvia.

"That's right, I remember, but why didn't you say no? I mean what was the point if I couldn't be there?"

"I did say no but actually it was a good thing I went. Ben's kids are really sweet." Jan turned back to her computer. "The little girl is kind of a brat but I made friends with Jack, his little boy."

Sylvia was quiet for a minute. "Well that's good. I hope you didn't throw up again."

"No, we didn't go on the Ferris Wheel or the Merry-Go-Round."

"Hello, Sylvia," Brent looked around the corner of the cube. "Did you have a good time with your family yesterday?"

"Yes,"

"Jan tried to call you to see if you would like to come to the park with us again yesterday but you were out of range."

Sylvia relaxed and stood to look at Brent under her lashes. "I couldn't have come anyway. My sister was visiting with her new baby and I couldn't wait to see him."

"If he looks anything like you, I'm sure he's adorable," Brent said.

Jan felt that sad feeling again but took a soothing breath while she listened to the exchange between Brent and Sylvia.

"He looks just like me." Sylvia smiled and sent a triumphant look to Jan. "Well, I guess I'd better get back to work." She swished her hips as she left the cubical.

"Jan," Brent said and her shoulders tensed. "I wanted to talk to you about the Foster account."

She relaxed. It was business as usual.

"Jan Dodd, account management," She answered the phone.

"It's me," Sylvia said.

"I know I saw you on the caller ID."

"Why did you answer so formally?"

"Force of habit,"

"Well, I just went to the water cooler to see if Brent was in his office and he isn't."

"So you went yourself for once instead of asking me to go check for you." Jan propped the phone on her shoulder and continued to type.

"Is he with you?" Sylvia asked.

"No,"

"Jan, are you ready for the budget meeting?" Brent asked from the entrance of her cubicle.

"Make that yes," Jan said into the telephone.

"Tell him you can't go to lunch. Tell him you have plans. Make something up. I'm going to ask him to go to lunch with me."

"Not today, we have a budget meeting." She held up a finger asking Brent to wait.

"Why don't I get to go to meetings? That would be a great way to impress Brent."

"If you work real hard maybe one day you will," Jan said. "Now I have to go. Have a nice lunch. Why don't we have dinner together tonight?"

"Okay, unless Brent asks me, of course," Sylvia said as she hung up the phone. She pulled her purse out of the drawer of her desk and looked around. She had an hour for lunch but there wasn't anyone else in the place she wanted to eat with. She sat at a small desk in a room full of them. Both accounts payable and accounts receivable were in this room. It felt like school the way all the desks were lined up in rows. When she first came she suggested they rearrange it but the people she worked with were such nerds.

She shrugged and left the room. She went out the door to the street and looked around. It was the first day of September but in Atlanta that was still hot. She didn't want to take a walk or she'd be sweaty for the rest of the day. Maybe she'd go to the mall where it was air conditioned.

"Sylvia, I'm so glad I caught you."

She jumped at the sound of her name and turned to see Jebediah Webb hurrying toward her from the parking lot. "You just barely caught me." She turned and started to walk down the sidewalk. "I'm going to the mall for lunch and maybe a little shopping."

"I wanted to take you to lunch." Jeb fell in beside her. "I tried to call but the receptionist at this place is a little slow. I described you to her as the tall gorgeous blond named Sylvia but she said there are two Sylvias that work here. Is that true? It's such an unusual name."

"Yes, there is another Sylvia in accounts receivable. I was surprised, too."

"Anyway, I couldn't tell her your last name because I didn't catch it when Brent introduced us the other night."

"I don't think he said it." She looked thoughtful. "In fact, I'm not sure he knows it."

"Well, what is it?"

"It's Kendall." She smiled and turned to look at him when they stopped at a cross walk. "I can't have lunch with you, Jebediah. I have an errand to run at the mall."

"Can't I come along?" He looked so sad that Sylvia smiled.

"I guess so."

The light at the crosswalk changed and they started across. "Did you notice that in flat shoes you're not taller than me?" Jeb hurried to catch up with her. "You do walk fast with those long legs of yours." He laughed.

She looked sideways at him.

"In fact," he continued. "I think I even have a couple of inches on you. I'm five eleven. How tall are you?"

"I'm five nine." She looked at him as he held the glass door to the mall open for her. "Does your height bother you?"

"No, but I thought maybe it bothered you." He looked sad again.

Sylvia went through the door and looked around at the food court. Her stomach growled loudly and she blushed.

"Sounds like we should eat first." Jeb laughed. "What was the errand you had to run?"

Sylvia looked around again. She didn't really have an errand to run. "I guess I don't have time to do that right now. I only get an hour for lunch and I'm starving."

"Were you just trying to shake me when you said that?"

"Of course not, let's go into the café. The food court is too loud." When they'd been seated and had ordered their lunch, Sylvia looked across the booth at the earnest face of her companion. "Jebediah," she said.

"Nobody calls me that but my mother." He smiled. "Even my dad calls me Jeb."

"Do you mind if I call you Jebediah?"

"No, I like it."

"Jebediah," she said again and noticed how his smile went all the way up to his eyes. In fact, Sylvia wasn't sure she'd ever seen anyone smile with their whole face like that. Yes she had. Jan smiled like that when she was working with the dogs and cats at one of her rescue projects.

"You wanted to say something to me?" Jeb prompted.

"Oh yes." She took a deep breath. "I really enjoy your company, but ..."

"But I should know that you're interested in someone else."

Sylvia sat back and frowned. "I'm that transparent?"

"It's Brent, right?" He sat back and frowned too. "You're pretty transparent but I have a lot of practice. This isn't the first time I've been attracted to a woman who couldn't see past Brent."

"And you still hang out with him."

"He's my best friend. He and Ben have been my best friends since we were in kindergarten." He leaned forward and smiled at her. "He can't help what he looks like any more than you can. It's probably the same for Jan."

Sylvia thought about it. "No, Jan really isn't interested in men. She had a few crushes when we were in high school but that's all. She hates to date. She says it's too awkward." Their food came and Sylvia laughed when her stomach growled loudly again as the plate was set in front of her. "I'm starving."

"I hope you don't eat like that all the time. A double cheeseburger and chili fries for lunch," Jeb said. "Your cholesterol must be off the scale."

"I take it you're some kind of health nut." Sylvia looked at his turkey burger and slaw. "Won't you be hungry half way through the afternoon?"

"Yes I will and I'll eat the fruit cup I have in the refrigerator back at the office."

"A fruit cup..." She soaked up the last of the chili with the last fry and popped it into her mouth. "Well, I won't have to because I ate a decent lunch."

"You know, you and Brent have a lot in common. He eats like a pig at lunch, too. I have a hard time talking him into having lunch with me because he knows I'll nag him. We're not getting any younger you know, Syl." He put his napkin in his lap and signaled the waitress for the check.

"Nobody calls me Syl but Jan," she said.

"Does it bother you?"

She looked at his earnest face again. "No, but that comment about not getting any younger bothers me, you have no idea how old I am."

"I'm guessing thirty five."

"Huhh..." Sylvia gasped. "How did you know that? I don't look my age. Everyone tells me I don't look my age." Jebediah Webb was definitely getting on her nerves. She wasn't ever going to see him again, she decided as she fumbled in her purse for her wallet.

"My treat." He waved his hand at her. "And I guessed your age by Jan's grey hair." He laughed and his smile was contagious. Sylvia relaxed and smiled reluctantly at him. "I ran into her running at the park yesterday. She told me that you two had been friends from kindergarten like Brent and I have. Otherwise I'd have guessed twenty-five."

"Now you're just being ridiculous."

Jeb paid the waitress and they left the mall and walked back to the firm.

"Why don't you go cycling with me on Sunday? We'll pack a lunch," Jeb said when they reached the steps to the building.

"Jebediah, I told you ..."

"I know, you're interested in Brent but he'll be there. We cycle together once a month and Sunday is our designated day. I'll suggest that he ask Jan and we'll make it another foursome. Even if you're not interested in a romantic relationship with me we can be friends. Can't have too many friends can you?"

"No, I guess not." Impulsively Sylvia kissed him on the cheek.

"Ewww..." He waved a hand back and forth in front of his face. "You shouldn't have had those onions on your burger. I wouldn't talk too closely to Brent this afternoon if I were you."

"That Jeb Webb guy is such a jerk," Sylvia said to Jan as she brushed her hair in the ladies' room that afternoon. "He insisted on coming to the mall for lunch with me today and then he had the nerve to tell me I had bad breath."

"Your breath really is bad. You had onions on your burger again didn't you?"

Sylvia glared at Jan in the mirror.

"And chili fries."

"I brushed my teeth. I even flossed." Sylvia put her brush back in her purse and turned to leave.

"It isn't your teeth. It's coming from your stomach. I'm sure there's an herbal remedy for it."

"I'll bet Mr. Smartass Webb knows what it is. He seems to be some kind of health nut."

"That's Dr. Smartass Webb and he probably does know."

"Jebediah is a Doctor?" Sylvia turned back around, "a Ph.D.?"

"Nope, an MD; Brent told me about him on Sunday. He's a doctor of internal medicine with a specialty in geriatrics."

"That's old people, right? Why would a young person specialize in old people?"

"We'll all get old sometime, hopefully." Jan opened the door and held it while Sylvia went out. "I guess you won't want to have dinner with me tonight, if you ate that much for lunch."

"No, I'll be hungry again by then."

"You know, Syl, someday your metabolism is going to slow down and you'll get fat. That'll be a real shock for you."

"That will never happen. I'm just naturally fit."

Thursday

"I just went to the water cooler to check on Brent and he's on his way to your cubicle," Sylvia said into the phone just as Brent walked around the corner and smiled at Jan. "Tell him you have lunch plans. I'm going to ask him to have lunch with me."

"But I don't." She smiled at Brent as he sat down on the stool next to her.

"You don't have to tell him what they are. Just tell him you have plans and leave the building. Take a lunch break for a change, JanJan. You work too hard."

"Alright," Jan hung up the phone and looked at Brent.

"Let's go to lunch." He smiled, flashing brown eyes and dimples at her. "You've worked through lunch every day this week."

"Oh, I can't do it today, Brent. I have an errand to run."

"Well, I'll come with you. Is it at the mall? We could grab something from the food court."

"No, I really have to do this by myself. I'm uhh, going underwear shopping."

Why did I say that? She thought as Brent's smile broadened.

"Oh I definitely want to come along."

"Well, you can't." She stood and turned around feeling the blush on her cheeks. She could feel her nose turning red.

"JanJan," Sylvia appeared in the opening of the cubical. "Oh hello, Brent." She smiled innocently. "I was just coming to ask Jan to go to lunch with me."

"She can't." Brent stood. "She's going underwear shopping."

Sylvia's eyes widened at Jan and she laughed. Then she turned to Brent. "Well, that leaves us both free for lunch. Why don't you have lunch with me? My treat, it was so nice of you to include me in the trip to Medieval Times."

"Well, I was going to tag along with Jan to the underwear store but she won't let me. Sure, I'd love to have lunch with you."

"Good." Sylvia smiled seductively. "Let me get my purse. I'll meet you at the front of the building."

"Alright," Brent said. "Maybe tomorrow, Jan, no, I have an appointment. I can't do it tomorrow." He put his hand on Jan's shoulder to stop her as she started to leave the crowded cube. "Oh wait, Jan. I almost forgot. Jeb wanted me to invite you to go cycling with us on Sunday."

"No, thank you," she said trying to push past Brent and Sylvia.

"Please? Sylvia will be there and Ben and Shannon are coming. The kids will be with Shannon's parents." He let go of her shoulder and she hurried past them and turned around. She looked at Sylvia who was smiling triumphantly.

"Come on along, Jan. It'll be fun."

"Well, alright. Do you ride far? I haven't ridden a bike for a while. I'm sure my tires are flat. How is your bike?" She asked Sylvia knowing that she didn't have one.

"It's in perfect shape." Sylvia smiled. She had rented one the day before.

"We can inflate the tires on your bike." Brent followed her down the hall. "We only ride about twenty-five miles, I mean both ways of course, but we don't have to ride that far if you don't want to."

"Twenty-five miles both ways," Sylvia and Jan said together but Brent had already gone into his office. They exchanged a panicked look then went in different directions.

"Oh, I'd rather sit at that table." Sylvia said opening her eyes wide at the host who seated them, "if that's okay."

"Sure, ma'am," the young man was obviously smitten. He led them to the corner booth that Sylvia had indicated instead of the table for four in the middle of the room.

"Thank you," Brent said as he slid into the booth. It was cozy sitting on either side of the corner.

"I already know what I want," Sylvia said.

"You've been here before? What's good?"

"I like the cheeseburger and fries," she said. The waiter came and she ordered. "No onions and no chili."

"I think I'll have the soup and salad," Brent ordered. He looked at Sylvia when the waiter had left. "Having a health nut for a best friend makes you think."

"Yeah, I had lunch with Jebediah earlier this week." It wasn't the health thing that had made her think. It was being accused of having bad breath. "So, Brent, tell me what made you want to be an insurance adjuster?"

"I don't really care what I do," he answered. "As long as it makes enough money to support my volunteer work and I can leave the job at the office when it's time to go home."

"Volunteer work?" She looked at him from under her lashes.

"Yeah, I work with the YMCA as a coach. I coach basketball and softball."

The man had more causes than Jan. Sylvia rested her chin on her fist as Brent talked about the work he did with several different children's groups. He wasn't talking about dogs at least. Their meal came and they ate in silence for a minute. Sylvia was glad for the break.

"So when did I lose you, Sylvia? Was it the Boys Club or the Big Brothers group?" Brent asked.

"You didn't lose me. I found it all fascinating," she said then laughed at his handsome smile. "You lost me somewhere between the two."

"So will you answer my question?"

"I will if you remind me of what it was."

"When do you go to the greyhound rescue on Saturday? I'd like to come and have a look."

"Oh, we usually get there about one o'clock. Jan loves to wash the dogs. The ones that come in from the track have never been cleaned so they need a lot of work. Of course, the ones that have been in the rescue for a while have to be treated for fleas and ticks."

"I'll have to check my schedule. If I don't have a game I'll come by. Will you answer another question for me?"

"What?"

"Why doesn't Jan have a dog? Jeb says that greyhounds make excellent apartment dogs."

"Listen, Brent." Sylvia looked at him seriously. "You heard her reasons the other night. I've worked really hard at discouraging her from getting a dog."

"Why, she loves them?"

"I can't stand the thought of her walking a dog in the middle of the night around that apartment complex and she would, you know." Sylvia sat forward and looked straight into his eyes.

Brent pushed back in his seat startled by the intensity of her look. "I hadn't even thought of that."

"Well, think about it before you suggest it to her again. You don't know Jan like I do. She would never ask that dog to wait. She'd be out there walking around the woods at all hours of the day and night, a babe in the woods. The thought scares me to death."

"Sylvia, you and Jan are really close friends aren't you?" Brent smiled.

"Since kindergarten, I let her think she takes care of me. Well, that's not true. She does take care of me but I take care of her, too. So don't suggest a dog again, at least not until she has a house." Sylvia took a deep breath. "And that scares me to death, too, but I don't think I can stop her."

Brent smiled. "Let's split a desert," he said. "Tell me about you, Sylvia. What do you like to do?"

Saturday

"I'm so glad you're coming with me today, Syl. It's been months since you've come to the rescue with me." Jan pulled on her waterproof boots and picked up her keys. "You look adorable." She looked at her beautiful friend. Sylvia had her straight blond hair pulled loosely to the top of her head and looped into a knot. She was wearing jeans and knee high rubber boots. Her t-shirt didn't quite reach her jeans exposing her flat belly. Her navel was pierced and framed by a heart shaped tattoo.

"It hasn't been months, JanJan. It's only been a couple of weeks."

"I guess it just seems like months because it's so much more fun when you come with me." Jan picked up her keys and headed for the door. "Did I tell you there are eight new dogs? They closed down a kennel in south Georgia. It was infested with Lyme disease. They had to put down a bunch of them but these dogs had negative tests. Their blood work looks good. I'm going to want one, you know."

"I know but these dogs have been rescued, Jan. They'll get homes."

"Yeah, you're right." They went out to the parking lot and got into Jan's car. "So how was your lunch with Brent yesterday?" She tried not to sound too interested. The truth was that she felt sad again when the two of them left together and she went alone to the mall. She actually bought underwear. She hated to lie to anyone.

"It was really nice toward the end," Sylvia said looking out the window thoughtfully. "He asked me to tell him about myself. He asked me what I liked to do and he listened like he was actually interested."

"You sound so surprised, Syl. Why wouldn't he be interested in what you like? Did you tell him about your painting and your sculpture?"

"Yeah, I did and he said he wanted to see some of my work." Sylvia frowned and looked at her hands in her lap. "It made me feel bad because when he was telling me about himself I was bored. I hate to say it, JanJan, but he's boring and worse than that, he's not the least bit sexy."

"You're kidding." Jan looked sideways at Sylvia and thought. I didn't think he was boring and he was definitely sexy.

"No, I'm not kidding. You know what, Jan. I think I might be wrong about this guy. Maybe I'm not interested. It's hard to believe with him being so good looking and all. I mean, I didn't eat onions or chili with my burger and fries because I was hoping he'd kiss me. By the end of the meal I was hoping he wouldn't."

"So I can quit arranging ways for you two to be together and we don't have to go cycling tomorrow?" Jan asked feeling somewhere between relieved and disappointed.

"No, I'm not giving up yet. Like I said, he's really good looking. Anyway I rented a bike. Maybe things will be different tomorrow."

They arrived at the rescue facility and Jan unpacked her absorbent towels. "Hey, ladies," Jeb said to them as they went through the door from the office to the groom shop.

"What are you doing here?" Jan asked.

"Where's Brent?" Sylvia asked.

"Brent was supposed to be here?" Jan looked at Sylvia. "So that's why you decided to come today."

"Brent had a softball game," Jeb said. "So show me around and tell me what you do. By the way you both look adorable."

Sylvia looked at Jan and rolled her eyes. Jan said. "First we'll find the owner of the place and ask her to show us the new dogs. It's really exciting today, Jeb. There are eight new dogs straight off the track. First we'll search them for ticks. Then we'll wash them, de-flea them, dry them and clean their ears."

Sunday

"These dogs are spectacular, Brent," Jeb said as he helped Sylvia adjust her bike seat. "There, try that." He held the bike steady while Sylvia sat on the seat. "Now stretch your leg. Your knee should be almost straight. That's good, take off." He let go of the seat as Sylvia peddled off. You look great," he called to her as he picked up his bike and hurried down the path to catch up.

"She does look nice." Brent pulled up beside Jan. "I like that biking outfit, Sylvia. You must ride often. You even have padded pants."

Jeb was beside Sylvia and behind them on the trail Brent rode beside Jan. Shannon and Ben had ridden ahead and agreed to wait for them at a designated lunch stop.

"I guess she must," Jeb said. "That bike is really nice but it looks well used.

"I love to ride bikes." Sylvia smiled obviously enjoying the attention.

Jan looked ahead at her best friend's tidy little bottom and felt hers spread over the narrow seat she had on her ten-year-old bike. The one she hadn't ridden in ten years. She had bought it on some fitness whim and had never liked it. It was a touring bike and the seat was higher than the handle bars. She had to lean over and look up and it always gave her a stiff neck and a headache. She groaned quietly as she felt her muscles starting to stiffen.

"Are you alright, Jan?" Brent looked at her concerned.

"I'm remembering why I don't ride bikes. I get a headache and my butt gets sore." She laughed. "Don't mind me. I may complain a lot but I run three miles five times a week. I'll keep up." She looked again at Sylvia. Her legs looked lean and toned beneath her spandex shorts. She rarely runs, she thought. As far as I know she rarely does any exercise. She'll poop out before me, I'm sure.

"So tell me about the dogs, Jeb," Brent said. "I'm sorry I couldn't be there yesterday, darlin. I had a game." He glanced at Jan.

"Well, you know what a greyhound looks like but did you know they come in all different colors?" Jeb continued.

"Well, no, I thought they were usually grey or maybe fawn colored."

"Yeah, they do come in those colors and they're beautiful but they come in all the different colors you've ever seen on a dog. There were even brindle ones."

"What's brindle?" Brent shifted his gears as they started a gradual climb.

Jan watched how he did it and tapped the same gear shift he had. She must have hit it too hard because there was a fast ticking sound and suddenly her legs were going a hundred miles an hour. She tapped the lever back again and the bike clicked again and she felt more pressure and was able to pedal but she'd fallen behind and Brent fell back with her.

"You have to shift a little more gently than that. Otherwise you change the gears too fast and these hills are so gradual that you can't ride in that gear," he said.

She felt her face turn red and pedaled a little harder to catch up with Sylvia and Jeb. She took a deep breath and pulled up behind Sylvia's tight butt again and noticed how her friend reached down to smoothly shift gears as the trail gently sloped downward. Jan had to put on her breaks. She couldn't even pedal.

"Shoot," she said. "I'm going to bump into you Sylvia. Move faster."

"Shift gears, Jan." Brent indicated his own gear as Sylvia and Jeb pedaled out of her way.

"I told you I hadn't ridden in a while," she said defensively.

"I know. Don't worry about it. You'll get the hang of it." He laughed as they settled back into an easy pace. "What's brindle?" he repeated.

"It's kind of striped, like a tiger or a tabby cat. They can have different colored stripes, too, like red and black or grey and red. You probably need to come and see one to really know." Jeb went on as if they hadn't had a near collision. "They can also be black and white, black or white. There was even one that was black and white speckled like a Dalmatian."

"I can come next Saturday," Brent said. "I want to see them."

"The only color I didn't see was merle. Do they come in merle, Syl?"

Jan winced when Jeb used her pet name for Sylvia.

"I don't know," Sylvia said. "Do they, JanJan?"

"I don't think I've seen a merle," she said. "But that doesn't mean there aren't any."

"What's merle?" Brent asked as they went over a bridge.

The trail was built on an old railroad track and Jan shuddered as they entered the bridge. She'd always been nervous on bridges. There were tall fences on each side for safety but when she looked over the edge of the bridge to a huge drop to the river below she screamed and the bike swerved. She hit the fence and bounced backward. Please don't let me knock anyone over, she prayed as she felt herself hit the wooden boards and slide to the other side of the bridge.

"Jan, darlin," Brent knelt beside her. "Are you alright?"

"JanJan, are you okay?" She looked up at Sylvia's anxious face then at Brent's. Behind them she could see Jeb looking at her with concern. She blinked and closed her eyes.

"Jeb, she's unconscious," she heard Brent say.

"She's bleeding!" Sylvia cried.

"Get out of my way, guys," she heard Jeb say. "Let me have a look."

"That's right. You're a doctor, thank God," Sylvia sounded like she was about to cry.

"Jan," she heard his voice close to her face. "Are you awake?" He pulled her eyelid down and she looked at him.

"I don't want to be," she whispered. "Actually, I'd like to crawl through the crack between these boards and fall to the river below."

"Well, you can't," he whispered back. "You're leg is bleeding and your fan club is about to get hysterical so we have to deal with it."

She glared at him. He was trying not to smile as he helped her sit up. "She's alright, guys."

"Oh, thank God."

"Come on, Syl," she said as she let Jeb help her to her feet. "You know I bounce. I'd have been gone long ago if I didn't bounce."

"What happened, darlin?" Brent was suddenly holding her around the waist and helping her to a bench.

"She has a terrible problem with heights and she's afraid of bridges," Sylvia said as she hurried along beside them. "I should have thought of that when I saw that bridge but I was having so much fun on the bike. I'm sorry, JanJan."

"Okay, you two," Jeb said. "I have a first aid kit in my pack but if you don't move away and give me room, I can't do anything. Why don't the two of you pick up the bike and see if it's damaged."

Sylvia and Brent reluctantly moved away from Jan and Jeb went to his bike and removed his pack. Jan watched as Brent and Sylvia picked up her bike and looked it over. This was the perfect opportunity for Sylvia to get some time alone with Brent. She looked down at her leg. It was bleeding on the side of her knee and she could see a splinter from the wood sticking out. She closed her eyes as a wave of nausea swept over her.

"Just don't look, JanJan," Jeb said. "I know about your weak stomach." He removed the splinter and bathed the wound with antiseptic.

"Ouch," she whispered.

"I'm sorry. I know it burns." He examined her knee making her move it in different directions and pressing on certain spots. "I don't think there's any real damage done. Do you want me to call for transportation for you out of here?"

"No, I'm fine," she said. "I can ride. Like you said, there's no real damage done."

"I feel terrible," Sylvia said to Brent. "I know she's afraid of heights. All we had to do is stop and walk our bikes over that bridge and she'd have been fine. It was the suddenness of it that threw her off."

"Don't feel bad, Sylvia." Brent picked up the bike and looked it over. "I know, too. She threw up on the Ferris Wheel last week. I should have thought about it."

"Is the bike alright?"

"Yeah, but the chain came off." He picked the bike up and carried it over to where all the others were stopped next to the bench. "Luckily I have a grease cloth in my pack so I don't have to get my hands all greasy." He worked on the chain for a minute until he got it back on track. "There you go. It's ride-able again."

"She can't ride back," Sylvia said surprising herself with her anger. "She's injured. How can you be so unfeeling?"

"I didn't mean she should ride it back. We'll call for assistance. This trail has assistance."

"I just don't see how you can be so concerned about a bicycle when ..."

"Oh, good, you fixed it." Jan limped up to them. "Let's go." She got on the bike and started down the trail.

Jeb picked up his bike and straddled it.

"She can't keep riding," Sylvia said.

"I think she can." Jeb pedaled off to catch up with Jan. "Don't be a hero, JanJan," he said as she hit a rough spot on the trail and struggled to balance the bike.

"You're right. I won't."

"So tell me what merle is," Brent said when they were sitting at a picnic table with Shannon and Ben. Shannon was pulling food out of her pack and spreading it nicely on the table. She even had paper plates and forks for everyone.

"What are you talking about?" Ben said.

"We were talking about greyhounds before Jan busted her leg and Jeb said he hadn't seen a merle. Do you know what merle is?" Brent laughed as he bit into a sandwich.

"Yeah, it's the color of our sheltie. Candy is blue merle but I think it comes in red, too."

"Oh, I see why that would be hard to describe."

"How did you bust your leg, Jan?" Shannon asked.

"I ran into a fence. I haven't ridden a bike for a while. I'm glad you've reminded me of how much fun it is." She took a bite of her sandwich and chewed. Everyone was looking at her and she was sure she wouldn't be able to swallow. Her legs were sore. Her neck and shoulders hurt from leaning down and looking up. Her butt hurt and her knee was throbbing. She smiled at the group of concerned faces, took a deep breath and swallowed with a gulp. I'm sure everyone heard that, she thought.

"How did you handle that bike so well, Syl," Jan asked when she was soaking in a tub that night.

Sylvia sat on the closed toilet and looked at her with concern.

"I mean, I didn't even know you liked to ride bikes."

"I didn't either, JanJan. I told you I rented that bike. Well, they offered a lesson with a rental so I had one yesterday. This really cute guy, a little younger than us but not too much, taught me all about the gears. JanJan, I just loved it. The feeling of gliding along that trail was fantastic. I hate that you fell on that bridge. It was my fault because I was so buzzed by the beauty of it I wasn't even thinking about you."

"It's not your fault that I fell, Syl." Jan ran a little more hot water into the tub and lowered her knee into it. She hurt all over.

"Are you sore? I mean you haven't ridden for a while have you?"

"No, I haven't and I am a little sore but it's a good sore." She stood and stretched. "I do think I'll go home and take a bath now that I know you're alright."

"At least my fall, no matter how embarrassing it was, gave you a little time alone with Brent," Jan said as Sylvia turned to leave the room.

She turned back and looked at her. "JanJan, I'm really sorry I put you through this," she said. "Brent's a jerk, a good looking one for sure but I'm not interested in him. I gave the bicycle coach my number. I'm pretty sure he'll call me. You don't have to find reasons to get Brent and me together anymore."

"Oh, that's good." Jan didn't know why she felt so sad.

"I appreciate what you've done for me, JanJan, all those trips to the water cooler to spy on him." Sylvia stooped beside the tub. "You even skipped Mass today to get me together with him on that bike trail."

"No I didn't. I went last night."

"Oh, well, I know you didn't want to go cycling today."

"I just don't understand why you were in such good shape." Jan slid a little deeper into the bubble bath. "I run. You don't do anything."

"I go dancing. Dancing is exercise too."
Sylvia kissed her on the cheek. "I love you,
JanJan. You're the best thing that ever
happened to me." She stood and left the
bathroom.

"You're the best thing that ever
happened to me, too," Jan said to the empty
bathroom as she heard the door to her
apartment shut and Sylvia's key turn in the
lock.

Wednesday

"I'm not taking no for an answer today." Brent stood at the opening to Jan's cubicle. "I felt terrible when I saw the way you hobbled around on Monday. I wish you had let me cook you dinner."

"I didn't hobble. My legs just felt like they wanted to go around in circles." Jan didn't turn from the computer screen. Brent had asked her to lunch and dinner on Monday and Tuesday and she had managed to tell him no and not give in when he persisted.

"You should have stayed home like Sylvia did."

"Sylvia shouldn't have stayed home. I think Mr. Baxter is already a little unhappy with her. She stays home too much. Sore muscles are not a legitimate excuse."

"Sylvia hates her job." Brent straddled the stool next to Jan's chair. "She needs to find something to do that she likes. She's much too artistic to be coding bills in accounts payable."

Jan stopped what she was doing and looked at Brent. His eyes were intense. He was really tuned in to Sylvia's needs. "You know," she said. "I've told her that a dozen times but school just doesn't work for Sylvia."

"I can see how it wouldn't. There are so many things you have to do in school that really don't have anything to do with your goal. I'm sure when Sylvia is excited about something she does it better than anyone else ever could."

Jan looked at him and took a deep breath. He never seemed to even notice Sylvia when they wanted him to, but he seemed to understand her as well as she did now. And I've known her for thirty years, she thought.

"I've tried to tell her she should be an entrepreneur. You don't have to have credentials if you're the best at what you do," Jan said.

"And I'm sure that Sylvia is the best at what she does. I keep telling her I want to see some of her paintings. Maybe you can convince her to show them to me," Brent said.

Jan looked at him for a minute longer then turned back to her computer screen. His face was so earnest it was uncomfortable. "Well, the problem is that if she can't hold on to this job, she'll be living on my couch again and the truth is, as much as I love her, we're better friends if we don't live together."

"I've got an idea." Brent brushed her cheek with the back of his fingers and she sat back startled. "Let's invite her to dinner tonight at my house with us. You can talk her into bringing a few samples of her work. I really want to see it. I'll invite Jeb. We'll be a foursome again. Okay?"

"Oh, I don't think so, Brent. Thanks for being so interested but I think Sylvia is probably otherwise engaged."

"You don't have to do a thing." He stood and kissed her on the top of the head.

What the hell? She could feel her eyes widen.

"I'll arrange everything. I'll talk to Sylvia and Jeb and I'll even suggest the art work. Don't worry about directions. I'll pick you up and bring you home. Seven o'clock, see ya." He left the cube and Jan looked at the computer screen. What happened?

"Give me five minutes and then meet me in the bathroom," Jan said to Sylvia on the phone.

"Why five minutes? I think if I sit here at this desk matching number codes to invoices for another second I'm going to blow. I mean the roof may blow off."

"Well, stop doing that then and watch your clock but don't come into the bathroom for five minutes." Jan stood from her desk and walked down the hall. The walls on either side definitely looked like they were getting closer together but she smiled and continued to the room labeled LADIES.

When she got there she went into a stall, pulled down her pants and sat down. She put her face in her hands and took a deep breath. The man wasn't quitting. The only reason she'd ever even talked to him was because Sylvia wanted her to. He'd asked her out because they worked together and she had to admit that in the year she'd worked for the firm they'd completed some projects together really well but it was just a mutual concern about the business.

"JanJan, are you in there?" Sylvia said as the door shut behind her.

"Yeah," she flushed the toilet even though she hadn't done anything. "Has Brent talked to you?" she asked as she pulled up her pants.

"He said good morning when I came in today. Why?"

"He told me that he wanted to see some of your art work. He's planning to get us together tonight. He's going to cook." Jan opened the door to the stall.

Sylvia jumped when she saw her best friend. "Jan, he hasn't threatened you or anything, has he?"

"Of course he hasn't." Jan took a deep breath. "Sylvia I'm scared, though, I mean not physically but he isn't quitting. I've turned him down for lunch and dinner on Monday and

Tuesday. Today he worked it so I couldn't turn him down."

"Don't worry, sweetie." Sylvia put her arms around Jan. "I'll just say I can't come tonight. Then you're off the hook."

Jan loved it when Sylvia hugged her. She was so much taller that when she hugged her Jan's cheek pressed into her shoulder and she felt so surrounded and so safe. She remembered Brent's kiss on her head and stiffened.

"No, Syl, if you say no I'll be alone with him. He said he'd pick me up. He's picked me up before. He knows where I live."

"Honey, you're really worried about this." Sylvia held Jan away from her by the shoulders and looked into her eyes. "Why are you afraid of him?"

"I'm not. It's just, well, you know, I don't want attachments, besides you. And I'd like to have a dog some day." She took a deep breath. "Sylvia, he's very perceptive. I think he's really interested in your art work. Why he wants me along I don't know."

"JanJan, I told you. He bores me. I don't want to encourage him anymore."

"Please, Sylvia, tell him you'll come. I'm scared to be alone with him."

"Hey Syl." She recognized Jebediah's voice when she picked up the ringing phone. "I guess you've heard about the dinner plans."

"Are you free for lunch today?"

"Yeah," he said. "You sound anxious. What's going on?"

"I need to talk to you. I'll meet you at the mall in twenty minutes." Sylvia pulled her purse out of the desk drawer and clocked out on her computer. She hurried to the mall and stepped inside the front entrance. She looked around. She hadn't designated where to meet before she'd hung up the phone.

"It's a big mall," Jebediah said from behind her. "That's what you were thinking, right?"

"Oh, I'm so glad you're here." She turned around and took his arm. "We should go into this restaurant where it's quiet enough to talk."

"What's going on?"

"I've made a terrible mess."

"What have you done?" They entered the restaurant and stopped talking while the hostess directed them to a table. When they were seated, the waitress came to take their order.

"I'll have a burger with fries." Sylvia glanced at Jeb, "no onion, no chili."

"No cheese, either," he said. "When was the last time you had your cholesterol checked?"

Sylvia scowled. "I will have the cheese," she said to the waitress. "My cholesterol is none of your business."

The waitress took Jeb's order of a veggie burger and steamed vegetables. "So what's got you so wound up?" he asked.

"Well, you know that I was interested in Brent, right?"

"You're not anymore?"

"No, he's really good looking but I find him boring. Anyway," she continued. "Jan was helping me get time to be with him. You know they work together. That's why I didn't have to worry about lunch today because they're in a meeting together."

"He loves those meetings with her. He talks about how efficient she is. He likes the way her voice is so soft but so confident." Jebediah smiled and sipped his water.

"Really, how long has he been talking about Jan?"

"Ever since she started working with him; I'm sure it's been over a year." He stirred his salad around to spread the dressing. "I've suggested that he ask her out several times but for some reason he was afraid to. Then when she started going to the water cooler and glancing into his office he thought maybe she would be interested."

"Oh no," Sylvia put her face in her hands. "She was spying on him for me."

"She'd go back to her office and call you to tell you that he was there and then you'd walk by in your mini-skirt, right?"

She glared at him. "Did he tell you that?"

"No, I guessed. I'm sure Brent didn't even notice. I think he's got it pretty bad for Jan."

"JanJan?" Sylvia looked at her cheeseburger and suddenly her appetite abandoned her. "So this isn't entirely my fault."

"No, in fact, you had very little to do with it."

"Well, that's even worse." She took a reluctant bite of her burger. "We've still got to stop it."

"Don't talk with your mouth full," Jeb said. "Why do we have to stop it?"

Sylvia finished chewing and took another bite. "Well," she said then stopped and looked at him. She finished chewing and swallowed. "You don't understand Jan. She's never had a relationship with anyone but me. I mean, she really didn't have very many friends in high school. It wasn't that nobody liked her. She just doesn't get comfortable with people very easily."

"I think she'll get comfortable with Brent. Everyone does." He leaned forward and made eye contact with Sylvia. "I think I do understand how you feel about Jan. Her innocence makes you want to protect her.

That's the way I feel about Brent, too, but I think we have to leave them alone on this."

Sylvia felt her heart start to pound at the intensity of his gaze. Why in the world was she feeling all fluttery? She took a drink of her soda then sat back and took a deep breath.

"Jebediah, please help me. Talk to Brent or something. Jan's scared to death. She really isn't interested in a relationship."

He leaned back and looked at Sylvia. He studied her face and she squirmed under his scrutiny. "You're really concerned about this, aren't you? I can promise you Brent's intentions are honorable."

"Jebediah, Jan just really can't handle this. She's very delicate. You've seen how I have to take care of her."

"I was under the impression that she takes care of you."

"We take care of each other."

"Mom, Dad," Jan opened the door to her apartment and let her parents in. "Did we have plans for tonight?" It was six thirty and she was just getting out of the shower. She was wrapped in her bathrobe and her hair was wet.

"No, we were just going out to dinner and we thought maybe you'd like to go with us," her mother said looking at her daughter. "Obviously, you'll need to dry off and get dressed."

"Hello, baby," her father kissed her wet cheek. "Go get dressed, we'll wait for you."

Jan looked at her parents. They were always so well put together. Her mother's white hair hung in layers to her shoulders and she was dressed in a perfectly fitting silk skirt and blouse. Her father's bald head shined and the hair around the side was trimmed close. His polo shirt looked brand new. They always looked brand new. Did he ever wear one twice? She put a hand to her wet curls and suddenly remembered what she was doing.

"I have some dinner plans, Mom, but I guess I could cancel them."

"Sylvia can come, too. Is she meeting you here or do we need to pick her up?"

There was a knock at the door and Jan jumped.

"Oh good, that'll be her." Her father opened the door and stepped back. "Who are you?" he asked as Brent entered the apartment.

Brent looked around the room with a smile. "I'm Brent Barlow. I've come to pick Jan up for dinner." He turned to Jan. "I'm sorry I'm a little early."

"Oh yes, well," she said. "Brent, these are my parents Fran and Thomas Dodd."

"I thought I saw some resemblance." Brent extended his hand to both of her parents. "You go ahead and get dressed, Jan," he said. "I'll entertain your folks."

"Can I get you some wine?" She heard Brent ask them as she went into her room and shut the door.

They were sitting in the living room sipping wine when she returned. "You were almost out of this stuff. You don't get any." Brent stood as she came into the room.

"That's probably just as well," her mother said. "She doesn't handle it very well."

"Good news," Brent said. "Your parents are going to come to dinner with us. I've made potato salad and baked beans. I'm planning to grill turkey burgers and veggie burgers. Jeb will be there and I don't want a lecture."

"You're coming along?" Jan felt stupid as she said it.

"Brent was kind enough to invite us and we accepted," her mother said. She approached Jan. "Apparently, Sylvia is going to show her work to him. We'll follow in our car." She took her husband's arm and they went out the door.

"They dropped by to take me to dinner," Jan said feeling stupid again and she felt short. Why was she so short when her parents were so tall? She watched her father open her mother's door for her. They were such a handsome couple. Where did I come from? She thought.

"That's what they said. I'm glad they're coming with us." Brent took her arm and guided her out the door. He held out his hand for her key. She gave it to him and he locked the door.

"Did you talk to Brent?" Sylvia asked Jeb when she opened the door of her apartment.

"When would I have talked to Brent this afternoon?" Jeb came into her apartment and took the portfolio case from her when she handed it to him. "I told you I was booked for the afternoon. In fact, I just got my last patient out the door. I haven't even been home yet."

"I was hoping you could at least call him."

"What was I going to say? Brent you can't go out with Jan. Sylvia won't let you."

"Of course not, you have to just explain to him that Jan is not right for him. She's not right for anyone. She has her life all planned out and the plan does not include a man."

"I think it would be better if you explained that to him, or better still, let Jan explain it." Jeb closed the door behind them and Sylvia locked it. He escorted her to his car and helped her put the computer case and portfolio in the back seat.

"She can't explain it. She'll get tongue tied and faint or something. We can't ever let it go that far." She put her hand on his arm. "You promised you'd help me."

Jeb looked down at her hand. It was small and the nails were painted. He looked at her face and smiled sadly. "You're sure you aren't just jealous."

"No." She smiled and removed her hand. The palm of it was burning a little and she wondered why. "I told you. I'm not interested in Brent. He's just too serious about things, all those causes. I'm bored when I'm with him, except when we're talking about me, of course."

"Yeah, Brent's a good listener." They rode in silence. Jeb pulled into a driveway and stopped the car. "It looks like we got here before they did." He helped gather her stuff and they went to the front porch of the house.

"His house is even boring." She looked at the red brick and the white trim. "So you'll help me get Brent to leave Jan alone?"

"I don't think you stand a chance of it, Sylvia, but I'll see what I can do."

"Just don't let him be alone with her until we've had a chance to talk to him."

"He's alone with her now," Jeb said as Brent's car pulled into the driveway and another pulled up to the curb.

Jan waved at Jeb and Sylvia who were sitting on the porch of Brent's house when they pulled up. It was a traditional southern house, two story red brick with steps leading to a broad front porch. There was a swing at one end and a bistro table and chairs at the other end. There were two rocking chairs in between. The front yard was just a stretch of lawn with a walkway up the middle.

"It's small but adequate," Brent said to her as they walked toward it. "Wait until you see the backyard."

"Franny and Tom!" Sylvia jumped up and ran to embrace Jan's parents. "Where did you come from?" She flashed a concerned look at Jeb. Was Brent already insisting on meeting Jan's parents? Why hadn't Jan said anything about it?

"We stopped by to take Jan out to dinner and I guess we walked in on your plans." Fran embraced Sylvia. "You look beautiful as always." She leaned close to Sylvia and whispered. "I assume Brent is your new young man. He's gorgeous." She pulled away and went to the house as Thomas put his arm across Sylvia's shoulders.

"So you're going to show us your artwork tonight," he said. "What an unexpected treat."

"Oh, yes." She looked around. Jeb was holding a computer bag and a portfolio case. He shifted the case to his underarm and extended his hand.

"I'm Jebediah Webb," he said.

"I'm sorry." Brent made the introductions. "Jeb is my best friend. He was kind enough to bring Sylvia over and help her bring her artwork while I went to pick up Jan. Come in everyone." He ushered them all inside.

"See, everyone just assumes I'm with Brent," Sylvia whispered to Jeb as they took her computer into the living room.

"I think that's odd since I brought you and Brent brought Jan."

"Yeah, but they don't think Jan's with either of you."

"What a lovely house," Fran Dodd said as she and Thomas followed them into the living room. Brent came in behind them and went to the back door.

"Come and look at the yard, Jan." He opened the back door and walked out onto a wooden deck that sat about two feet off the ground.

Jan smiled at the people in the room and followed him out. The rest of the group went too and they all gathered on the deck.

"I think it's the perfect yard for a greyhound. What do you think, Jan?" Brent stepped down the single step to the yard below. He took Jan's hand and pulled her along with him.

Jan looked around the back yard. It was fenced all the way around with a wooden privacy fence. "How big is it?"

"The whole property is three quarters of an acre but the house sits forward on the lot so I think the back yard is about half an acre." He smiled down at her.

"Are you planning to get a greyhound?" Sylvia stepped down to where they stood and wedged in between them.

"Eventually," Brent smiled at Sylvia then turned to open the grill. "I'll start the fire. Jeb would you offer everyone whatever they want to drink." He turned back to his guests. "We'll have dinner then we'll look at Sylvia's work. Jan says you have a slide show on the computer."

"Yes I do," Sylvia said. "I put it together with music. It'll be fun."

"I'm really impressed, Sylvia," Brent said when they'd finished looking at the computer slide show.

"I am, too, honey," Thomas Dodd said. "I knew you were good but I didn't realize you were a genius."

Sylvia beamed at the praise. "I had a lot of fun putting together the slide show."

"The music went with the art work perfectly and the way you have it displayed in your apartment is great," Jeb said. "Have you ever thought about interior design?"

"That's what I keep telling her," Jan said. She felt uncomfortable sitting on a wooden bench chair with Brent. They had set up the computer so that it displayed on the white wall over the dining room table. When Jan had sat down on the bench her mother had been sitting there but she'd moved to the couch with her father when they had started the slide show and Brent sat down next to her. Sylvia sat in a chair at the head of the table and Jeb was in an easy chair next to Jan's parents.

"Her apartment is really nice. I was impressed when I picked you up this evening," Jeb said. "I wish I'd had a little more time to look at it."

"Thank you." Sylvia grinned widely.

"I want to see the sculpture," Brent said. "The paintings you have in your portfolio case are excellent. The pictures of the sculpture work are good but I'd like to see the real thing."

"Well, I have a few in my apartment but most of them are at my parent's farm in Danielsville. I have a studio in the loft of the barn."

"Sylvia, have you ever thought about asking one of the local art galleries to sponsor a show of your work?" Jeb asked.

"Do you think anyone would want to? Do you really think it's good enough?"

"Yes, I do."

"What about interior design, Sylvia?" Fran Dodd asked. "Don't you think you'd be happier in a field like that than what you're doing? We all expected Jan to go into some kind of desk job but with your spirit it must be just killing you."

"Thanks, Mom," Jan whispered. Brent reached for her hand and squeezed it. She jumped slightly and looked at him. He was smiling at her.

"Interior design is a very competitive field." Sylvia responded. "I don't have credentials. No one would hire me."

"Be an entrepreneur, Syl," Jan said. "I've been telling you that for years. If you're your own boss you don't need credentials."

"What am I supposed to do, just hang out a sign? People will still want references."

"Get references," Brent said. "What do you think of my interior design?" He gestured around the room they were sitting in.

Sylvia blushed and Jan gasped. She'd never seen Sylvia blush.

"Tell me the truth."

"It's boring."

Brent roared with laughter and Jeb joined him. "That's what Jeb says. All of my furniture came out of somebody's basement and the few pictures that I have are hung on nails that were already in the wall when I moved in. I've got an idea. I'll be your first customer."

"Really, you'd hire me?"

"Sure but don't get carried away. Remember I'm a boring guy. I work at a desk job like Jan and I'm perfectly happy with it."

"Well, that's part of the designer's job, matching the design to the customer." Sylvia jumped up and down. "Oh, I'm so excited."

"I am too, honey." Fran stood and Thomas stood with her. "I think we'll go on now. We have a business to run in the morning."

"Thank you so much for including us tonight." Thomas extended his hand to Brent.

"Brent, can I look at some of your picture albums and walk through the house to get an idea of who you are?" Sylvia was still so excited that she was bouncing.

"I think that would be great but not tonight. I think Jan needs to go home. She likes to be well rested for her work day," Brent said after he'd seen Fran and Thomas to the door.

"Let me help you with the dishes, Brent," Jan said as she picked up the glasses from around the room and carried them to the kitchen.

"No, I'll do them later. I'll take you home now and Jeb can take Sylvia." Brent looked at Jeb. "Maybe she'll invite you in to get a better look at her apartment."

"We can drop Jan on our way, can't we Jebediah." Sylvia elbowed him in the ribs.

"Uhhhg..." he said. "Of course, there's no reason for you to go out Brent. You've got dishes to do."

"No, I'm taking Jan home." Brent came out of the kitchen tugging Jan behind him. "I'll do the dishes later. Sylvia, we'll get together tomorrow and figure out what the next step is. I had a great time tonight. Thanks for coming, you two." He helped Jeb pick up the portfolio case and the computer and herded them out the door. He locked it behind him and they went to their separate cars.

"You should have insisted on taking her home," Sylvia said when she and Jeb were in the car.

"I tried. There was no way Brent wasn't going to take her home."

"What's he going to do, kiss her or something?"

"You sound so terrified, Sylvia. Do you think Jan has agonized every time she thought a man might be going to kiss you?" he said. "Do you think Jan's never been kissed before?"

Sylvia was silent. Why was she so upset about the idea that Jan might actually find a man. Was she jealous because she'd set her sights for Brent and he wanted Jan? Was she really that selfish?

"Don't beat up on yourself, sweetheart." Jeb put his hand on her arm and it burned where he touched her. "I know you love Jan. It's clear that you want to protect her. I'm sorry I said that."

"So why am I so panicked about him taking her home? I really think that I know how innocent she is, Jeb. I don't think she can handle being in love with someone." She looked out the window. "And I suppose the fact that I wanted him and she got him bothers me to some degree."

Jeb pulled into the parking lot of Sylvia's apartment complex. "So can we stop trying to keep them apart?"

"I don't know. I'll let you know tomorrow."

"Can I come in and look at your apartment?"

"Not tonight. I have a lot of thinking to do."

"Can I come in?" Brent said as he unlocked Jan's apartment door.

"Like you told Jeb and Sylvia, I like to be well rested for my work day." She smiled and held out her hand for her key.

"Just for one glass of wine." He held on to the key.

"I thought you said I didn't have any wine left."

"I lied," he said. "I hardly ever lie and I hardly ever manipulate a situation. I have rules against that kind of thing but tonight I broke the rules." He smiled at her and she felt her knees go weak. "Please let me come in for one glass of wine. You can have one, too. Your mother didn't let you drink any at dinner."

Jan laughed. "She's very protective of me and you've seen that I don't drink very well." She went through the door and closed it when he was through it. She held out her hand for her key and locked the door behind him.

"I'll get the wine." Brent went into the kitchen.

"You've become very comfortable in my apartment." She followed him in.

"Your apartment is very comfortable."

"Sylvia decorated it while she was living here of course."

"I figured." Brent poured the wine, picked up both glasses and went into the living room. "She did a really good job. The place looks like you."

Jan followed him into the room and looked around. Brent sat on the couch, put the glasses on the coffee table and signaled for Jan to sit beside him.

"It does look like me but I could never have done it." She sat on the couch at the opposite end. He moved over beside her and handed her a glass of wine.

"I don't drink very well, Brent." She put the glass down on the coffee table.

"You don't have to drink anything if you don't want to." He sipped his wine and put it down on the coffee table next to hers. "Wine was just an excuse to come in here and sit on the couch with you."

Jan picked up her wine and sipped. "It was nice of you to hire her."

"Who?"

"Sylvia,"

"Oh yeah, Sylvia; I'm sure she'll do a good job and she really needs to find something to do that she'll enjoy doing. She hates the job she has now."

"I know, Brent, but I can't just support her for the rest of her life."

"No, you can't." He took the glass out of her hand and put both hers and his down on the table. "And you can't keep using her as an excuse to avoid me either." He touched her cheek and leaned forward to kiss her.

Jan tried to turn away but he wouldn't let her. He kissed her lips and held the pressure for a minute. Then he touched her tongue with his. She tried to pull away but she suddenly felt like she was attached to him somehow and their tongues and lips pressed firmly together. Brent put his hand on her back and pulled her close. There was nothing she could do. She was lost in him. She melted into his chest. He moved his lips away from hers and she felt cold. Then he kissed her jaw and her neck just below her ear and she felt warm.

"I love you, Jan," he whispered.

"What!" Jan snapped to alert and blinked her eyes.

"I do, Jan. I have forever."

"You haven't known me forever. In fact you don't know me now." She put her hands on his chest and pushed him away.

"Okay, I did that too fast. I'm being overwhelming again." Brent sat back and picked up the glasses of wine from the table. He handed Jan hers and she took a gulp. "Don't drink it that fast." Brent took the glass away from her. "It's my fault. I moved too fast. I don't want you to make yourself sick."

"Brent, why did you say that?"

"What?"

"That you love me."

"Because I do, I loved you the first time I saw you. Then when you talked in that interview I knew it wasn't just what you looked like. Your voice is so soft and yet so firm."

"Not just what I look like?" Jan thought of her reflection in the mirror. She was short. Her hips were a little too big, her breasts a little too small. She had curly to frizzy black hair streaked with white.

"No, it isn't just because you're beautiful, Jan. I swear."

She looked at him. His eyes were boring a hole in her and the cleft in his chin quivered. "Well, that's nice but, Brent, I'm pretty sure you don't love me."

He looked at her for a minute. "Well, alright for now. Did you hate my kiss?"

She took a calming breath. "No, it was very nice."

"Good." He stood and pulled her to her feet. He walked her to the door. "I'll do it again then," he said and leaned down to kiss her. He was so tall that she had to turn her face up to him. For a second she felt like Scarlett O'Hara kissing Rhett Butler. She opened her eyes and he was smiling at her, their lips only a fraction of an inch apart. "I'll see you in the morning," he whispered and then he was gone and the door was shut behind him.

"Lock the door, Jan," he called from the other side.

Friday

"This is entirely your fault!" Jan said to Sylvia as they sat down at the picnic table outside of the building where they worked.

"I can't believe you're speaking to me again." Sylvia unpacked her sandwich. "You even packed me lunch. You didn't say a word to me yesterday. You wouldn't even pick up my calls."

"Yesterday went by in a blur." Jan bit into her sandwich. "Sylvia, Brent told me he loved me. What am I going to do?"

"Well, just tell him you can't return his feelings," she said. "And don't talk with your mouth full."

Jan stuck her tongue out at Sylvia. It was coated with bread and mayonnaise.

"Gross," Sylvia laughed and closed her eyes.

"I told him I wasn't interested and he said he'd just moved too fast and he promised to slow down. He didn't say he'd leave me alone. Then he kissed me again."

"Was it good, the kiss I mean?"

"I guess so. I don't have much to compare it to." Jan took another bite of her sandwich and looked at Sylvia.

"Well, did you enjoy it, dummy?" Sylvia laughed.

"Yeah but it made me forget what I was doing. I'm not used to forgetting what I'm doing."

"So let me see if I understand this." Sylvia put down her sandwich and leaned forward to look at Jan across the table. "When he kissed you, you forgot what you were doing?"

"Right,"

"Did you remember where you were?"

"Not until he said he loved me. Then it was like someone splashed cold water in my face."

"Hmmm..." Sylvia looked pensive. She picked up her sandwich, took a bite and chewed thoughtfully.

"Syl, you're not going to believe it. He said it wasn't just because I'm beautiful." Jan put her hand on her chest. "Me!"

"JanJan, you are beautiful."

"You only feel that way because we're such good friends. People you love always look beautiful." Jan took the last bite of her sandwich and washed it down with a swig from her water bottle.

Sylvia looked across the table at her friend of thirty years. It was true that she loved Jan and that certainly made her look nice to her, but she was pretty in her own right, too. She just played down the way she looked. Sylvia suddenly felt guilty. She played her own looks up partly to show up Jan. Why did they play this little game? What does it really matter what you look like?

"I can't believe I let you get me into this mess."

Sylvia bristled. "You know, Jan, this isn't completely my fault. Jebediah says Brent's been talking about you ever since you came to work here." She picked up her trash and stood to throw it in the can angrily. "Did you ever think maybe Brent is attracted to you? Maybe he has loved you from the beginning. You said it yourself. Everyone looks beautiful to the people who love them."

"What are you getting so mad about? I'm the one in a mess."

"You're in a mess because a handsome man who is just as boring as you are has fallen in love with you. I hate to tell you Jan but a lot of women wouldn't define it as a mess." Sylvia turned and stormed into the building.

"Now *you're* not picking up *my* calls." Jan sat down on the stool on the other side of Sylvia's desk. She'd tried to call her all afternoon. She finally gave up and went to the accounting department to talk to her.

Sylvia looked up from the calendar in front of her. She was drawing a scene in the blank square that represented this day. She scowled and looked back down.

"You shouldn't be drawing, Syl. Don't you have work to do?"

Sylvia made a production of pulling the stack of bills out of her inbox and opening her code book.

"Why are you so mad at me?" Jan demanded.

Sylvia looked up and met her eyes. They held her gaze for a minute then she looked back down at the bill in front of her. "I don't know."

"Well, try to figure it out. I don't like it when you're mad at me."

Sylvia wrote a code on the bill then put her head down on her desk. "I hate this job."

Jan sat back and took a deep breath. "It was the only one I could get for you, Syl. We'll watch for something better." She leaned forward and put her hand on Sylvia's arm. "Let's go out to dinner tonight, just the two of us. We haven't done that in a while."

Sylvia sat up and looked at Jan. She took a tissue from the box on the corner of her small desk and blew her nose. "Isn't this your vegan fast day?"

"You saw what I had for lunch. I cancelled the fast for today. Come on, it'll be fun. Then tomorrow we can go to the rescue together."

"You have everything planned out, Jan. What time will you go to Mass on Sunday?"

"Noon, you can come with me to that, too." Jan smiled. "We haven't been to church together for ages."

Sylvia smiled sadly. "I can't do any of it. I'm going out to dinner tonight with Vance and tomorrow I'm going for a bike ride with Jebediah."

"Who's Vance?"

"He's the guy I told you about at the bike shop, remember, when I rented the bike. He gave me a lesson."

"Oh yeah, the young one,"

"I don't think he's much younger than me."

"What about Mass on Sunday?" Jan stood. For some reason she felt very sad.

"I'll let you know. I don't like to think that far ahead."

"Come on, Sylvia," Vance said as they stood outside her apartment door. "Just let me come in for one beer."

"I think you've had enough beer." She steadied the young man as he staggered and bumped into her. "Here's your cab." She pointed Vance in the direction of the cab that had pulled up to the curb. She had driven home from the sports bar they'd had dinner in. He'd ordered two pitchers of beer. Sylvia could drink a glass or two but then she was full. Vance had finished the rest. By the time the sporting events he was loudly enjoying were over she was sober and he was roaring drunk.

"What about my car?" Vance slurred as she poured him into the back seat of the cab.

"It'll still be here in the morning."

"How will I get over here?" He rolled the window down when she closed the door and leered at her. "Maybe I should stay the night."

"That won't be necessary. If you can't get a friend to drive you, call me. I'll come and get you. Goodnight, Vance." She called to the half open window as the cab pulled away.

She hurried to her door and picked up the phone to call Jan. She wanted to describe the miserable evening she'd had. Glancing at the clock on the mantle she put the receiver back down. It was one o'clock in the morning. Jan would be sound asleep. With all the plans she had for the weekend, Sylvia didn't want to interrupt her sleep.

Jan looked at the clock on the bedside table. It read one o'clock am. She'd tried to call Sylvia at about midnight but she still wasn't home. She was sure she was out partying with Vance, probably having a wonderful time.

She sat up and turned on the light. She was usually sound asleep by now but Brent had called her at ten pm. He apologized for calling so late but he had just arrived back home after being gone to a job in south Georgia since Thursday. She'd wondered why he wasn't at the office for those two days.

Why had he called her tonight and why was she so happy to hear his voice. She couldn't go to sleep for thinking about it and she couldn't sleep with Sylvia mad at her. Her stomach ached and she felt bloated. She'd eaten a hamburger for dinner. She hadn't cancelled her Friday fast for years.

"What happened to my perfectly organized life?" she asked out loud as she picked up a book off the table and tried to read.

Saturday

"JanJan!" She turned at the sound of Sylvia calling her name. "Wait for me." She was running at the park. She'd gone about a mile and was already feeling winded.

"You don't realize how important a good night's sleep is until you try to go without one," she said as Sylvia caught up to her and they resumed a slow jog.

"You didn't sleep well last night?"

"No, I can't sleep when you're mad at me."

"I couldn't sleep either," Sylvia said. She panted slightly with the exertion. "I don't run very often so excuse the shortness of breath."

"Why are you here? Are you meeting Vance or something?" Jan looked around her.

"No, I called your apartment and you weren't there so I figured you were here."

"You came to see me?"

"Yeah, I started to call you last night when I got home but it was too late. I'm sorry, JanJan. I don't know exactly why I acted so stupid yesterday but I know I did."

"I did, too," Jan said as they slowed a little more to round a bend in the path. "This stuff with Brent isn't your fault. It's just so confusing to me. I've never had to deal with anything like this before."

"Has he asked you out again?"

"No, he called last night to tell me that he's been out of town on business and that's why he hadn't been at the office. Now why do you suppose he felt the need to do that? Why is it any of my business?"

"I think he really might be in love with you, JanJan," Sylvia said. "Which may be one of the reasons that I acted stupid yesterday, I'm jealous."

"I'm sorry, Sylvia. I really didn't plan to take him away from you."

"I never had him. How could you take him away from me?" Sylvia laughed. "Besides I'm not jealous of you, I'm jealous of him."

"What do you mean?"

"I just never thought of you as having a partner. I always thought I'd have you to myself. I mean who will take care of me if you're taking care of someone else."

Jan slowed to a walk and put her hand on Sylvia's arm. "Nothing will ever come between us, Syl. You've had hundreds of boyfriends and nothing ever came between us. Not that he's my boyfriend, not that he ever will be."

"So you don't have feelings for him?" Sylvia hated the hopeful sound of her voice.

"Like I said, I'm completely confused." They walked in silence for a minute.

"How was your date with Vance last night?" Jan broke the silence.

"Terrible, he took me to a sports bar where he was able to watch three sporting events at once, in between trying to grope me, of course. He ordered two pitchers of beer. You know that stuff fills me up before I get a buzz so he got completely snockered. I had to call him a cab and pour him into it. All the while he was trying to talk me into letting him spend the night instead."

"I'm sorry."

"He called just before I left the house. I have to go and get him so he can pick up his car. I also have to go to the bike shop and rent another bike. You know what? I think I'll buy one. I really did enjoy that bike ride."

"So you're really going cycling with Jeb today. I thought maybe you'd made that up just to get out of going to the greyhound rescue with me."

"No, I'm really going cycling."

"Good." Jan stopped at her car and put the key in the lock. "Can I give you a lift to your car?"

"No, it's right over there behind that big rock." She pointed. "I kind of enjoyed that run, JanJan. Maybe I'll do this with you again some time."

"You're not mad at me anymore?" Jan sounded so desperate that Sylvia smiled.

"I don't think I was ever mad at you, JanJan. I'm just a little confused, too. Maybe we're having our mid-life crises."

They both laughed. "Does that mean we have to have another one when we reach mid-life?" Jan asked.

"Who knows, we both seem to be full of surprises."

"Who are you?" Jeb demanded when Sylvia pulled into the parking spot at the bike trail with Vance in the passenger seat and two bikes on the back of the SUV.

"I'm sorry, Jeb," Sylvia said as she got out of the driver's seat and went to the back of the car to remove the bikes. "I made the mistake of telling Vance that I was going to the bike shop to rent another bike and he insisted on coming along, which is actually a good thing because my car wouldn't start. This is his SUV."

"That still doesn't answer my question. Who is he?"

"I'm Vance Long." The burly young man held out his hand to Jeb. "I'm Sylvia's boyfriend."

Jeb shook his hand and looked questioningly at Sylvia.

"He's not my boyfriend for heaven sake. We went out last night and I thought that would be the end of it, but like I said, he insisted on coming along this afternoon."

"You know you're crazy about me, Sylvia." Vance lifted the bike off the rack with one hand and put it on the ground next to Jeb. "We got chemistry."

Sylvia rolled her eyes. "Anyway, the good news is," she pushed the bike to the trail and fastened her helmet. "I bought one of these bikes today. This isn't it. I rented this one because I had to order the one I wanted. I wanted a custom paint job on it. Isn't it beautiful, Jebediah?"

She looked at Jeb. He was staring at Vance with his eyes narrowed slightly. He looked at her and she stepped back. The look on his face was scary somehow. Was he angry? Was he hurt? He clearly didn't like Vance.

He shook his head as if to clear it, then he said. "Uh, yeah, that's great. What color is the custom paint?" He pushed his bike beside hers and threw his leg over it.

"It's teal. Teal looks so nice with my coloring." They mounted their bikes and started to ride. "I got a helmet to match and a new riding outfit. It'll be here in a week. I can't wait."

"Pick it up, guys," Vance said as he whizzed past them. "I say we do fifty miles today, both ways."

"Don't worry, Jebediah." Sylvia smiled sideways at him as she shifted gears to pick up speed. "He's actually pretty controllable."

"Jan, I'm glad I caught you," Brent's voice called from the parking lot as she locked the door to her apartment. "I thought we could ride over together."

"Brent," she said as she turned and walked toward him with her bag of bathing supplies. "I'm sure I didn't make plans with you for this afternoon. I always go to the greyhound rescue on Saturday afternoon."

"I know. I'm going with you. Remember last week when we were riding bikes I told you I didn't have a game today so I could come by." He took her bag and put it in the back seat of his car. "Get in." He opened the passenger door for her.

"I usually get pretty dirty washing those dogs. Are you sure you want to come back from there in your Jaguar?"

"It's just a car, darlin. In fact I didn't even buy it. I inherited it from my dad."

"Is your father deceased?"

"Yeah, he died two years ago." Brent pulled the car out of the parking space. "I came along kind of late."

"Oh, I'm sorry."

"I miss him a lot." Brent smiled sadly. "I have a brother twelve years older than me and a sister ten years older but I think I was the closest to my dad. He left most of what he had to me. We redistributed it evenly but I kept the car."

"What about your mother?"

"She's still alive but they were divorced."

"Oh," Jan thought about her parents. She would hate to lose either of them. She would hate it if they split up, too.

"Don't feel sorry for me, Jan. That's not why I told you that. I have a loving family even if I do miss my dad."

"I wasn't feeling sorry for you. I was just appreciating my own parents."

"Good. I liked them too. Do you have any brothers or sisters?"

"No, well I guess Sylvia is like a sister."

"Yeah, she's like a pesky little sister to me."

"Why do you say that?"

"She's always trying to get between you and me. Does she think I'm not good enough for you or does she just want you all to herself?"

Jan looked at him sharply. His eyes were on the road and he was frowning. She wanted to say. No, you dimwit, she wants you to notice her instead of me.

"No, she's just protective," she said.

"Well, what does she think I'm going to do to you anyway? My intentions are honorable."

Jan laughed. His intentions are honorable. Did he come from some time in the past?

"Here we are," he said as he pulled into the parking lot of the rescue facility.

"Hey, Dee," Jan said as they entered the kennel. "Do we have any new dogs this week?"

"No, but the dogs that you washed last week are itching again. You know it usually takes a couple of weeks to get all the ticks and fleas off and the entire kennel needs treatment." The owner of the facility looked past her to Brent.

"Oh, Dee, this is Brent Barlow. He's going to help me today. Sylvia couldn't make it."

"Another Friday night party? I don't know how she does it. Isn't it time for her to start slowing down. She's no spring chicken, you know."

Brent laughed and Jan covered her smile with her hand.

"Well, I think you should start with that big brindle with the scar on the middle of his back. He seems to be suffering more than the others." Dee pointed into one of the runs. "He's limping on his right front foot. I think there must be a tick in one of the pads of his foot. I was just about to check it out."

"We'll check it out." Jan opened the run and led the dog by the collar to the wash tub. She scooped the dog up by his middle and put him in the tub.

"Whoa." Brent rushed to her side. "You shouldn't lift that dog, Jan. He's too heavy for you."

Dee laughed. "I don't think we've ever had a dog in here that she couldn't lift. She may be small but she's dynamic. I'll leave you to it, Jan. Shout if you need anything." The owner of the facility left the kennel and Jan fastened the dog's collar to the lead on the tub.

"I checked these dogs pretty closely last week," she said. "But ticks can start out so small that you miss a few. In a week's time it could have swollen up and caused serious irritation, maybe even infection." She picked up the dogs foot and felt between the pads with her fingers. "Yep, look at that."

"Yuck." Brent looked over her shoulder. "That tick is huge."

"Yeah, I'm going to look him over before I pull it out. He might not let me do too much and I want to get them all today if I can." She picked up his other front foot.

"How did he get the scar, Jan?" Brent stroked the beautiful dog's back. The scar zigzagged across the dog's back for about three inches then down his side.

"I don't know for sure but I think it's usually from the starting gate at the race track. Either that or he got snagged on a kennel. They live pretty tough lives on the race track."

"I've heard they get way overpopulated and only the best dogs make it to the track."

"That's right." Jan moved on to the dog's back feet. She picked each one up and inspected.

"I don't suppose there's any way to shut the tracks down, is there?" Brent followed her progress looking over her shoulder.

"No, the industry is too big and even though it's been very corrupt, I think they're trying to work with us. Our best chance is to get them to participate in our rescue projects." She stood and stretched her back. "Okay, he has four in his feet. Let's look at his ears." She examined both ears and said. "Two more, I'll start with this one. Brent would you hand me my bag."

She reached back to point to where she had put the bag down and felt her elbow collide with something.

"Ahhh," Brent gasped.

Jan straightened and whirled around. Brent was holding his eye. "Oh no, what did I do? I'm so sorry. I didn't realize you were so close behind me." Jan looked up at him and took his arm. "Let me see it, Brent."

"No, just leave it alone, Jan. Man, you sure are a dynamo. Ouwww." He clutched his face and turned away from her.

"Brent, don't be silly, let me see it." Jan followed him around as he tried to avoid her. She grabbed his arm and pulled his hand away from his eye. He was squinting and the eye was watering but there wasn't any swelling yet.

"I'm fine, Jan. It's just excruciating pain that will go away in a minute. So, just leave me alone and get on with your work."

"No way, Brent, you need to soak that eye with ice or something."

"No I don't. We have ticks to pull out of that dog and a whole kennel worth of dogs to give flea treatments to." He looked down at her. He was obviously trying to open his eye all the way but failing. "Now let's just get on with it."

Jan looked at him and scowled. "Well, alright, be a hero," She reached inside her bag and pulled out a hemostat. "We'll get on with it."

"Are you finally going to let me put something on that eye? It was no fun watching it swell up all afternoon while we washed and flea treated twenty five dogs." Jan unlocked the door to her apartment and went inside with Brent right behind her. "It's turning a lovely color of black and blue now. What will you say happened?"

"I'll tell them my girlfriend punched me."

"I thought you said you rarely lie."

"Okay, my girlfriend hit me in the eye with her elbow."

"I'm not your girlfriend." Jan pulled an ice pack out of the freezer and indicated for Brent to sit at the table. She stood in front of him and pressed the ice pack to his eye.

"You loved that big brindle dog with the scar, didn't you?" Brent asked.

"Yeah, in another year I'll have a down payment on a house. First thing I'm going to do is get one of those dogs."

"But that one will be gone. What was his name, Diesel?" Brent took the pack from her and she sat down across from him at the table.

"Yeah, he won't be adoptable for a while but I'm sure he'll be gone long before I can afford to buy a house."

"I have to agree with Sylvia, though. I don't want you walking a dog in the middle of the night around this complex."

"That's not why I don't get one. It's because it wouldn't be fair to the dog. Is that why Sylvia is so dead set against me getting a dog?" Jan stood up and walked to the window. She looked out at the wooded grounds of the apartment complex. "This place is perfectly safe. You know, maybe I should look into that dog. Sylvia is protective to the point of controlling sometimes. I just need to draw the line."

"No, I mean, I think Sylvia said something about it not being fair. You know they are big dogs. No, Jan, he needs a place to run, you know stretch his legs." Brent followed her to the window. "Why won't that dog be adoptable for a while?" he said trying to change the subject.

"What?" Jan looked up at him over her shoulder. "Oh." She went back to the table and sat down. Brent followed and sat down beside her. "He goes in to be neutered next week then they like to put them through an obedience class. You know these dogs haven't been socialized in any way."

"Dee said he'd already tested small animal safe," Brent said. "How do you test him small animal safe?"

"They're sight hounds and as racing dogs, they're trained to chase things. Some of them will kill small animals. That's why I don't have a cat. I don't want to risk my greyhound hurting it, when I get a greyhound that is."

"How do they test them? Do they torture some poor cat?" Brent put the pack back on his eye.

"It sounds like torture but these cats and small dogs are never in any danger and they know they aren't. Dee has a Yorkshire terrier and a couple of cats, her personal pets. They're in a room protected by two layers of fence. If one of the greyhounds strains at his leash to get to them, we don't recommend he go to a home with small animals."

"So what is small animal safe?"

"If the dog looks interested but not excited we recommend keeping them separate when not supervised. When they're being supervised we recommend a cage muzzle for the dog until small animal safety has been established. If the dog shows no interest, we're pretty confident. But we recommend caution until the pets have established a relationship. Let me see the eye." Jan pulled the pack away from Brent's face. "Ohhh, I'm so sorry." It was swollen shut now and the black and blue had spread around the eye. It was starting to turn yellow in spots.

"I don't care. Thanks for taking me along today."

"You took me."

"Let me take you out to dinner."

"No," Jan said. "I owe you. I'll cook."

"He's not so hard to get rid of after his second pitcher." Sylvia laughed as she opened the door and she and Jeb went into her apartment. "I appreciate you following us to his place so I don't have to go and bring him to his car again in the morning. I was starting to think I'd never get rid of him."

"No problem. I'm just glad he didn't argue about letting you drive." Jeb sat down on the couch and looked at the painting over the mantle.

"Would you like something to eat? I noticed you didn't eat any of the chicken wings or cheese fries Vance ordered at the sports bar."

"You didn't eat them either. How about I take us out to a nice quiet place for a healthy meal?"

"Do you know of any such place?"

"You bet I do. We can even get a glass of wine."

"That sounds nice, Jebediah. You've been a good sport today. Thanks."

Sunday

"Hey, JanJan." It was Jeb's voice she heard when she picked up the phone first thing in the morning. "I'll bet you're about to leave to go for a run in the park."

"I'm that predictable?"

"Absolutely, I'll meet you by the gym and we'll run together, okay?"

"Sure, I'll be there in about fifteen minutes." She hung up the phone and walked out the door. He was right. She had been about to leave.

Jeb was sitting on a brick wall outside the park entrance when she pulled up and got out of her car. "I brought water." He held up two eight ounce bottles of water and handed her one. "I noticed last time that you didn't have any with you."

"I hydrate before I run." Jan took the bottle of water from him.

"That's probably alright but it's better to have some with you and hydrate while you run." They started up the path at a gentle walk then slowly increased their pace to a jog.

"I usually do this alone. I've had company two days in a row now." Jan laughed. "Sylvia ran with me yesterday morning."

"Really, I don't see Sylvia as a runner, too full figured."

"Oh, and since I look like a palm tree with hips you see me as a runner."

"I did not say that." Jeb laughed. "You're just more compact. That's the way runners look."

"Sylvia has long legs. Don't runners have long legs?"

"It isn't just body style that makes me think she's not a runner. It's attention span, too. Running requires some focus. I don't see Sylvia as having much focus."

Jan was silent for a minute. "That's definitely true. I think that's why she has such a hard time holding a job."

"I don't think she'd have a hard time holding a job if it was the right job."

"Probably not, but what is the right job? I swear, Jeb, I've tried everything."

"Has she tried anything?" They turned a corner and he slowed down. "I'm not much of a runner myself," he puffed. "I'll try not to slow you down too much."

Jan slowed her pace and glanced sideways at him. "Yes, she's gotten herself several jobs but they never last. She has a really hard time being on time and she likes to leave early and take long lunches."

"What kind of jobs has she had?"

"Mostly similar to what she has now. She's been a hostess in a couple of restaurants. Waitressing didn't work. She doesn't tolerate the irate customers. Dumping a glass of water on someone's head tends to get you fired, no matter how much he deserved it."

They both laughed.

"No artistic jobs?"

"No, honestly, I think she's terrified of criticism. You know how sensitive artists are."

"Yeah,"

"I hate putting her in a place where she's miserable but I can't support her for the rest of her life. Her family loves her but they have this thing about tough love. They think if they make her live on the street she'll figure out something to do with her life."

"You've talked to them about it?"

"Yeah, they think I should abandon her, too. I can't. If, I guess I should say when, she leaves this job, for whatever reason; she can live on my couch. It'll be nice when I have a house. At least then I can give her a bedroom." She picked up her pace and ran ahead of Jeb for about a mile then slowed and let him catch up to her.

"Man, you can really run," he said. "Do you run marathons?"

"No, I never have, maybe someday." She was feeling powerful. "You know it's funny but I don't ride a bike well at all. Did you notice how well Sylvia rode when we went last week? She doesn't even work out."

"I think life is a workout for Sylvia," Jeb said and they laughed again. "But that's what I was saying about body type. Sylvia is just built for riding a bike, not for running. Brent and I are the same. I can way outride him but he runs marathons and he usually places."

"He does?"

"Six a year, marathons are twenty-six miles you know."

They ran the rest of the trail in relative silence. "I usually go around twice," Jeb said. "I have focus. I just can't run very fast." He laughed. "But I have to pick Sylvia up for mass so I'll stop now. She said the two of you were going to the noon service."

"Funny, she didn't tell me that."

Jan rushed into her apartment and picked up the ringing phone. "I'm going to mass with you," Sylvia said. "Jebediah and I will meet you at the front of the church at eleven forty five, okay?"

"That's great, Syl. I saw Jeb at the park this morning running. He mentioned that you and he planned to come with me."

"Oh really, good, see you in a while." Jan hung up the phone and it immediately rang again. "Hello."

"It's me, darlin," Brent said. "I'll pick you up in twenty minutes to go to mass."

"You're coming, too?"

"Yeah, we'll have lunch afterward at my brother's restaurant. I hope you haven't eaten much."

"No, I just had juice when I got up."

"Good."

"That was a beautiful service," Jan said as they sat down at a table in the restaurant around the corner from the church. "I love that priest. He's always so upbeat."

"What happened to your eye?" Jeb said.

"I wondered when you were going to ask about that." Brent smiled. His eye was almost swollen shut but you could see a small slice of brown and white in the slit between his lids. "Jan punched me."

"Tell the truth or I will punch you." She laughed and Sylvia's heart pounded. She'd never seen Jan act so comfortable with anyone before, anyone other than her.

"Ron," Brent said as a man with similar dimples and of similar build approached the table. His hair was considerably greyer than Brent's but the resemblance was remarkable. Brent stood and embraced him.

"What happened to your eye?"

"Where's Mom?" Brent asked, obviously ignoring his question.

"Here she comes." Ron gestured to a woman approaching from behind Brent.

He turned around and embraced a tall thin grey haired lady. "Honey, what happened to your eye?"

Brent laughed again and turned back to the table. "Let me introduce you to my friends. You know, Jeb, of course."

"Hey, Ron, Sally." Jeb stood and extended his hand. He tapped Brent's brother on the arm as he shook his hand. "I've heard great things about your restaurant. I can't wait to try it out."

"It's good to see you Jeb."

"This is Sylvia Kendall." Brent continued. "She works in our accounting department at the firm."

Sylvia smiled exposing her large straight pearly white teeth. "It's so fun to know the owner. I've been here before, at night of course. This place rocks."

"I'm glad we've made a good impression."

"And Ron, Mom, this is the woman I've been talking about for the last year and a half." Brent turned to look at Jan and her breath caught in her chest. The look in his eyes was something she'd never seen on anyone's face before, not when they looked at her. He almost glowed. "Jan, this is my mother Sally

Smith and my brother Ron ... Barlow, of course."

"I am so pleased to meet you, Jan. For a year I've been saying to Brent. When will I meet your girl but he just kept putting me off." Brent's mom said.

I'm not his girl. Jan thought.

"Did I tell you that Mom and my brother own a restaurant together, Jan?"

"No." She couldn't say anything. She didn't know she would be meeting his family today. She looked around. Hadn't he said something about a sister?

"If you're looking for my sister, don't," Brent said. She lives in Savannah with her husband and kids.

"Oh, good," Jan's hand went to her curly hair. She had worn it loose around her shoulders and only pulled back the top. She always wore it that way to mass. She didn't know why but for some reason she felt uncomfortable. She looked up at Ron. He was smiling at her and Brent was pulling her to her feet.

"It's nice to meet you, Jan. I thought I'd gotten thoroughly sick of hearing Brent talk about your voice and your hair and all the things he loves about you but seeing the way it makes him glow I decided I could listen some more." He took her hand and squeezed it between both of his.

"Oh,"

"Let me plan the menu for everyone today." Ron looked around the table and Jan slid self-consciously into her seat. She could feel her cheeks flaming. Brent sat down beside her and took her hand to squeeze it under the table. She felt her nose light up. "Is anyone allergic to anything?" Ron asked.

"JanJan can't eat scallops." Sylvia said.

Jan looked at her sharply. Was she always so protective? Sylvia looked sad. A moment before she had looked excited at meeting the owner of the restaurant. What happened? Brent's mom had called Jan his girl. Brent made the comment about him talking about her and Ron backed it up with his response. Did Sylvia still have a thing for Brent or was she just jealous of the attention. That was entirely possible.

"No scallops then," Ron said. "Anything else?" He looked at Jan.

"Other than that I can eat pretty much anything." She noticed her voice squeaking. What in the world did Brent like about her voice?

"What do you think, Mom?" Ron asked, "The salmon or the filet?"

"I'll think about it when I know what happened to your brother's eye." She looked back at Ron. "You two haven't been fighting again have you?"

"No, Mom," Ron said. "I haven't given him a black eye in ages. In fact, I don't think

I've ever given him one. I was twelve years old when he was born, remember?"

"That's right," she said. "It was your sister that gave you a black eye," she said to Brent.

"No, she gave me one, Mom." Ron laughed.

Brent said, "So what are you going to serve us for lunch? Do you prefer Salmon or filet, darlin?" He squeezed her hand under the table again.

"What happened to your eye?" Sally demanded.

"I punched him," Jan said then slapped her hand over her mouth.

"I thought Brent's mom was going to give *you* a black eye. I guess that maternal protectiveness never goes away." Sylvia laughed as the four of them walked to their cars. "What possessed you to tell Brent's mom that you punched him, even if you did?" She looked back and forth between Brent and Jan. They looked guilty and she bristled, "What did you do to her to make her need to punch you, Brent," she demanded.

"Whoa, get back," Brent laughed. "Talk about protective."

"It was an accident, Syl. He just sort of ran into my elbow with his eye."

"I think it's more like you ran into my eye with your elbow."

"Yeah," Jan grinned easily again and Sylvia's heart thumped. "That is more accurate."

They arrived at the place where they had to split up to go to their separate cars. "Let's go for a hike, guys," Brent said. "The weather is perfect and we can walk on one of those paths down by the river."

"I think that sounds like a great idea," Sylvia said. "Only I want to ride bikes again. I don't have to return my rental until tomorrow. Did I tell you about my new bike, JanJan?"

"A couple of times." She looked at her friend's glowing face. "I'm glad you've found something you enjoy so much."

"I don't think Jan wants to ride again," Jeb said. "I looked at the knee when we ran this morning. It might be worse than I thought. It's really black and blue."

"It's not so bad but I still can't do anything this afternoon," Jan said. "I've volunteered to go to a new cat rescue facility."

"You're not going to wash cats are you, JanJan?" Sylvia said. "That sounds dangerous."

Back off, Sylvia, Jan thought. She took a deep breath. "I'm not going to wash cats, although, I would if they needed me too. I'm sure that some of the rescued cats need baths.

But I volunteered to help with socialization. In other words, I'm going to pet them."

"The three of us could still go for a hike or a ride." Sylvia looked hopefully at Jeb and Brent.

"I think I'll go to the cat rescue with Jan," Brent said. "You two go on and have a good time."

"We don't have to go, Jebediah," Sylvia said when they were driving home together. "I'll have a bike of my own next week. I can ride any time I want to."

"Let's go, Syl, please? I'll take you to your apartment. You can change your clothes and we'll load your bike. I have the rack on the roof. Then we'll go to my house and get my stuff. I really want you to see my house anyway."

"Okay, good, I really want to go for a bike ride."

"But you don't care about my house."

She looked at him. He was smiling but it didn't quite reach his eyes.

"Of course I do. I want to see your house."

The phone was ringing when they opened the door to Sylvia's apartment. "Hello." She picked it up. "Oh, hello Vance," she said. "No, I'm going somewhere this afternoon. I can't ride with you. Thanks anyway."

"I really need to get caller ID." She laughed when she hung up."

"You do." Jeb was scowling. "Go ahead and change. I'll take the bike out to the car."

Twenty minutes later they pulled up to a large house in an upscale neighborhood. "It's beautiful, Jebediah." Sylvia jumped out of the car as soon as it had come to a complete stop. She walked to the middle of the lawn. "I can't believe you live here all alone. It's huge."

"Do you like it?"

"It's beautiful. It's a dream house. Can I go inside?" She looked at him hopefully.

"Of course, you didn't think I'd make you wait on the front stoop, did you?" Jeb laughed and led her up the walk to the front door. He unlocked it and stepped back for her to go in.

"You haven't lived here for very long, have you?"

"I've lived here for five years." Jeb chuckled. There's furniture in the kitchen, the sun room on the back of the house and the master bedroom. I have a bed in one of the other bedrooms for my nieces. I usually only get one at a time but it's a trundle just in case."

They walked through the large empty foyer then the large empty living room. The large empty dining room was visible from the hall and they entered the large full kitchen.

"Oh," Sylvia said on a breath.

"I like to cook. It's set up perfectly for the attention deficient cook. In fact, I'm thinking of writing a book called the ADD kitchen."

"Why? You're not ...?"

"I like to think so, yes. Spectacular people ... ADD's, never dull."

"They called me that in school. I hated it." She turned a circle looking at the large kitchen and knowing exactly how to cook in it. "I've never been much of a cook but I think I may be able to in this kitchen."

"I designed it myself." He walked over to the state of the art refrigerator and opened the door. "Here," he handed her a water bottle. "It clamps onto your bike. I'll go change." He started up the stairway.

"Where does the stairway in the entrance go?" she asked.

"Same place, I have a front staircase and a back one."

Sylvia uncapped the bottle and took a drink. She looked around the room. There was a fireplace in the end of the room. There was a love seat and chairs facing it and a flat screen TV on the wall next to the fireplace. On the other side was a door to a sun room. Sylvia went out and stood at the wall of windows to the backyard. It was big and fenced but not landscaped.

"I plan to put a pool out there and a hot tub but I just haven't gotten to it. I work too much." Jeb came into the room and stood behind her. She turned around and found him very close. Their mouths were only inches apart. She wondered what it would be like to kiss someone so close to her height. She'd always dated tall men.

For a minute she thought he would kiss her but he turned and went back into the kitchen. "Ready to ride?" He picked up his water bottle and went through a door into the garage.

She followed him. She was disappointed. Why didn't he kiss her?

"Hello, Jan." They were greeted at the door of the facility by a small man with thick glasses.

"Hey, John, this is my friend Brent." She introduced them and they shook hands. "He's going to pet cats with me today."

"Good, we can use all the help we can get." John turned and went down a hallway with Brent and Jan behind him. "I thought I'd put you in with this new litter of feral kittens we have. They've been here for a couple of weeks and we're not getting very far with them. We need a concentrated effort. You said you'd come a couple of times during the week too, right?"

"That's right, Tuesday and Thursday. I can leave a little early and come straight here. That way I can spend rush hour here instead of in traffic." She glanced at Brent. "I cleared it with Mr. Baxter."

"I know. Dan talked to me about it. He's very happy with your work." He followed her into a room that smelled only slightly like a dirty litter box. "You could ask for just about anything right now and he'd be fine with it."

"Could I ask for a raise for Sylvia?"

"I said *you* could ask for anything, not Sylvia."

"I just cleaned the boxes in here," John said. "The smell will dissipate soon. I get the best results from sitting on the floor. The chairs are still really foreign to these cats."

"I don't see any cats." Brent looked around.

"They're in here. It's time for them to eat." He handed two cans of cat food to Jan. "Sit down on the floor and put the bowls in front of you. That usually gets them out here." John left them alone in the room.

"Let's sit side by side over here in front of this overstuffed chair. That way we'll have something to lean back on." Brent sat down and leaned against the chair. He stretched his arm up to Jan and she handed him a can of food and sat down cross-legged next to him. His legs were stretched out in front of him and her knee brushed against his thigh.

She stiffened and looked at Brent. He didn't seem to notice. He was opening the can and scooping it into the bowl beside him. She opened her can and put it in a bowl in front of her crossed ankles. They sat back and waited.

Brent put his arm across Jan's shoulders and kissed her cheek. She smiled shyly and blushed. "Look," he whispered in her ear and pointed to the chair across the room. The face of a half grown kitten edged the skirt of a chair up and looked out then another one then a third. "How many are there?" He kept his voice low.

"Just three," Jan whispered. "That's all of them. John said they're about five months old. They're feral, wild."

The first kitten to show its face slowly moved out from under the chair and cautiously crossed the room. The others followed it to the bowl in front of Jan. They all put their faces into the bowl to eat and a chorus of purrs started. They were all three pure black with eyes a deep yellow almost gold looking.

"Males or females, do we know?" Brent asked softly.

"Females, all three."

Jan smiled and reached toward the boldest kitten. She stroked it lightly on the back and it raised its tail into the air. She smiled at Brent and he smiled back. "You're beautiful when you smile like that, Jan."

She felt herself blush again. She leaned over to pet the other two kittens. They shied away just a little then allowed her to stroke them. She very gently reached under the first kitten's belly and lifted it into her lap.

Brent reached over to pet the kitten and the purring became louder. He smiled and Jan saw his dimples and felt herself blush again. Her nose was definitely getting red and she looked down at the kitten in her lap. Brent reached to pet the other two kittens. They finished the food in the bowl and lay down next to his leg. They all looked at Jan and Brent with wide frightened eyes then slowly started to clean themselves.

The kitten in Jan's lap moved to Brent's lap and Brent picked it up and held it against his chest. A car horn blew from outside the window and the kitten scrambled up Brent's shirt and on up his face, over his head and disappeared behind the chair. All the kittens were gone in a flash.

"I feel awful," Jan said as she bathed the scratches on Brent's face. "Look at your shirt, it's covered with blood. You must have scratches on your chest, too." She started to unbutton his shirt then stopped when he put his hand on hers and squeezed.

"My chest is fine." They were back in her apartment. They had left the rescue facility with a wet cloth pressed to the scratches on Brent's face and heartfelt apologies from John. "That blood is from my face." Brent smiled. "Don't worry about it, Jan. I'm fine but," he smiled at her and kissed the hand he held in his. "I guess you can take off my shirt if you want to."

Jan sat back and looked at him. He was sitting on her couch and she was kneeling beside him. There were three scratches on his left cheek. One of them cut right through one of his dimples. They weren't very deep. They probably wouldn't scar. She'd bathed them and disinfected them then smeared antibiotic cream on them. But they still looked angry. Of course his right eye was still black. "I've made a terrible mess of you," she said.

"It was worth it to see you smile the way you do at the animals. You really love those creatures. I wish you'd smile at me that way."

"Brent," Jan sat back on the couch and put her legs over the side. "We need to talk."

"I don't like the sound of that."

"I don't really understand how this all started but it just isn't going to work."

"Why won't it work? I love you, Jan. I have for as long as I've known you. Honestly, we have a good time together. I even think you had a good time the first night we went out, even though you threw up on the Ferris

Wheel. Now that we know, we won't go on Ferris Wheels, right?"

"Yes, but I'm just not looking for a relationship." She looked at him sharply.

"You don't want a relationship or you don't want me? Whatever isn't right about me I'll change it if I possibly can. What don't you like about me? Tell me, Jan."

She looked at his face. His eyes met hers and she could see his question in them. There was nothing wrong with him. He was perfect. He was beautiful and he really seemed to love her. They enjoyed the same kind of work and the same kind of recreation. What was wrong? Why wouldn't this work? It wouldn't. She'd always known it wouldn't.

"I don't like the way you're looking at my face." Brent smiled. "I can't change the way I look, Jan, but you'll get used to it. I have. I hated those dimples when I was a kid. You know how vain kids are. Here I was this tall skinny boy with this fat face but I've gotten used to it. You will, too."

Jan laughed out loud. He really doesn't know how handsome he is, she thought.

"There you go. I love it when you laugh. It tinkles like a bell ringing." He put his arm around her shoulders and pulled her close. He tipped her face up with a finger under her chin and kissed her. "Jan when I kiss you don't you feel a rippling low in your belly," he whispered. "I do, actually all I have to do is touch you to feel it. Sometimes I only have to look at you."

"I thought it was gas." She bit her tongue.

Brent laughed. "No," he said and kissed her again. "It's your loins."

"I didn't plan this," she said against his lips. "A relationship, I mean."

"I did. Isn't that enough? I know you like to have a plan, so why don't you just use mine."

"When did you plan it?"

"Somewhere between meeting you and taking you to Medieval Times, I even bought that house with you in mind."

Jan felt her eyes widen.

"But if you don't like it, we'll sell it and choose another one together. I promise I'm going to learn not to be so overwhelming."

"I love that house. How could you have known I would?"

"I'm telling you, Jan. We're part of a bigger plan. We're supposed to be together. I believe it, can't you?" He kissed her again and she forgot what she was doing. She forgot where she was and she forgot why this wasn't going to work.

Wednesday

"I have to say." Sylvia stood at the entrance to Jan's cubicle. "This has been a very humbling experience."

"I swear I didn't plan this, Syl. Who would have ever thought Brent Barlow would choose me. What does he see in me?" Jan sat with her elbows propped on her desk and her face resting on her hands.

"He sees the beautiful loving person that I've known for thirty years." She sat down on the stool beside Jan. "Besides my vanity being a bit ruffled, I think the hardest thing for me is knowing that I won't have you all to myself anymore. I mean, now that he is officially your boyfriend."

"He's my boyfriend," Jan repeated with a smile. "That sounds so nice."

"I think this must have been humbling for Brent, too, judging by the condition of his face. You've really done a job on him. If you want to get along with his mother, I'd keep him away from her until he heals a little." Sylvia laughed. "So has he asked you to marry him?"

"No, he said he bought his house with me in mind but he didn't say anything about marriage."

"I hope he knows how old-fashioned you are."

"If he doesn't he'll learn." Jan turned to her computer and booted it up. "How did the bike ride go with Jeb on Sunday? I think this is the first time we've talked since then."

"Yeah, see what I mean about sharing you. It went okay except that we ran into Vance on the trail. Jeb told him that he wasn't invited to join us. I mean he said it just like that but Vance still stayed with us the whole time. This guy is starting to creep me out, Jan."

"What do you mean?" Jan turned from her computer and looked at Sylvia with concern.

"I told him I had plans that afternoon but he showed up at the bike trail. We even went to a different trail this time. Was that just a coincidence?"

"Well, I suppose it could have been. He's a bicycle jock. He probably goes to all the different trails."

"Yeah, but I seem to be running into him all over the place these days. He was at the mall yesterday when I went at lunch time to get a manicure and pedicure."

"You can't get a manicure and pedicure in an hour."

"That's true. I don't think anyone has noticed that I take long lunch hours but old man Baxter was standing at the front door when I came in 45 minutes late this morning. I don't know if anyone has noticed that I leave early, though." Sylvia stood. "Anyway, Vance has called me every day this week several times each day."

"Have you told him you're not interested in him?"

"Yes, but he just keeps saying something about chemistry. Honestly, I don't think he's very bright and not only that but he's a lot younger than I thought he was. "He's only twenty four years old."

"Shouldn't you be at your desk, Ms. Kendall?" They both looked up as Dan Baxter spoke. Jan jumped. She hadn't even heard him approach.

"Oh, yes." Sylvia slithered by him. "I was just discussing one of the invoices with JanJan, I mean Ms. Dodd." She sneered at Jan from behind his back and hurried away.

"Ms. Dodd," he said. "Could you come to my office for a minute? There is a little matter I need to talk to you about."

"Alright, just let me finish what I'm doing here and I'll be right in."

Uh oh, he's going to fire Sylvia and he wants to give me a heads up, she thought. Well, at least she has two weeks to figure out another way to make rent. She can give notice at her apartment and start sleeping on my couch in November.

She locked the keyboard on her computer and hurried down the hall to Mr. Baxter's office.

"Come in and shut the door," he said. "Have a seat." He indicated the chairs across the desk from him. "Ms. Dodd, it has come to my attention that you and one of our vice-presidents have become somewhat involved."

"Involved," Jan repeated.

"Romantically involved," he said. "That's against policy."

"People aren't allowed to fall in love with each other? I didn't think that was something you could control." Jan felt anger building behind her words and resolved not to let it show.

"Maybe not, but I can control who works in this firm. It's mine. I'm the president and I will not have it turned into some kind of soap opera." He sat back and looked at her. "You're very good at what you do. I would hate to lose you. You've done wonders with your accounts and you are so efficient that I've been able to eliminate one of my account managers which saves me a lot of money."

Jan looked at him but said nothing.

"Brent Barlow is very good at what he does, too. In fact he's a little too good. He's so in control that some of the employees look to him for answers that they should be looking to me for."

Why had she never realized what a buffoon this man was? "So what are you saying?"

"I'm saying that if I make Brent Barlow choose between you and this place, he'll choose you. Then you can stay here and you can still have Brent Barlow. Don't worry. He won't have any trouble finding something else." Dan Baxter leaned forward and looked into her eyes. "I'd have to have some kind of agreement that you wouldn't quit to have babies or anything like that."

"So this policy is new. It hasn't been against the rules for people to fall in love before."

Mr. Baxter's face turned red and he blew his cheeks out in anger. "Surely you see the wisdom of it. How can a business run properly when the employees are romantically involved?"

"My parents have worked together all of their married lives, very successfully, I might add, in both their marriage and their business."

He leaned back again and looked at her.

"Why do you want to get rid of Brent?" she asked.

"I don't own this business alone," he said after a cold stare.

"Oh, I see. Brent makes a little too good an impression on the partners."

"He's a flashy show off." There was a pause in conversation while they stared at each other. "I'll accept your resignation today, then," he said. "You see, they did agree with the policy on romantic involvement. Two weeks will be sufficient notice. Write a letter of resignation and have it on my desk by the end of the day."

"How does that help with the problem with Brent?"

"He'll be so mad, he'll quit. He'll have some idea that he can start his own firm. Mark my words. He'll be right behind you."

As Jan left the room she heard him pick up the phone and dial. "Ms. Kendall, I'd like to see you in my office, please."

"He fired me." Sylvia was crying when Jan opened the apartment door to her. "I'm sorry, JanJan. It's all my fault, of course."

"Of course it was." Jan pulled Sylvia into her living room and put her arms around her. Sylvia's tall frame melted and they ended up on the couch holding each other.

"I was late all the time. I did more art than work. I took long lunches."

"You hated that job," Jan said. "I should never have put you in a position like that."

Sylvia pulled away and looked at her. "I hated that job but you were only trying to help me. You're always trying to help me but you can't because I'm just too stupid."

"Don't ever let me hear you call yourself stupid again."

Sylvia looked at her for a minute and sniffed. "You know, I went to look at Brent's house to decorate it and he'd done some research on decorating prices. He showed me what it costs and he offered to pay me midrange. It will cover my rent for next month but I'll have to give notice and move back in with you in November."

Jan was silent.

"You know my parents won't help. They love me enough to let me suffer for my own good, remember."

Jan was silent.

"JanJan, are you alright?"

"Yeah, I'm just wondering who's going to pay my rent."

Sylvia was silent.

"He fired me, too." Jan said. "Well, he demanded my resignation."

"Oh no, was it because of me?" Sylvia started to cry again.

"No, it was because there's a policy against romantic involvement between employees."

"I don't ever remember hearing about a policy like that."

"It's new."

"So, he wanted to get rid of you."

"No, he wanted to get rid of Brent but I wouldn't let him."

"What are we going to do, JanJan?"

"I don't know but I'll think of something." The bell rang and Jan opened the door to Vance.

"Come in, son," Thomas Dodd said when he opened the door to Brent Barlow that evening. "I can't tell you how nice it was to have dinner at your house the other night." He paused and looked up at Brent. "What happened to your face?"

Brent went into the warm living room and sat down. "I've been doing cat and dog rescue."

"Oh, I suppose Sylvia roped you into helping with that. Those girls have always loved animals."

Fran came into the room with a tray of crackers and cheese. "Can I get you a drink?" she asked. "Oh, dear, what happened to your face?"

Brent laughed and waved her question away. "I could drink a beer if you have one, or a cola."

"Which one," she said going behind the counter of a wet bar in the end of the room. "Beer or cola?"

He cleared his throat. "A cola would be nice."

"You know, Sylvia has been a part of this family since she and Jan were five years old," Tom said.

"That's right." Fran handed him a glass with a knit coaster around it. "We even took her on vacation with us when they were growing up. That way Jan had someone to play with and we didn't have to entertain her. Everyone got a break."

"They are very good friends." Brent took a sip of his cola. "I admire that about them. You know I would never try to come between that."

"No, I'm sure you wouldn't," Fran said. "I could tell that you and Jeb are that close."

"Yeah, we're kind of a threesome. We have another member. Ben is married with children so we don't see as much of him but we're still very close."

"That's wonderful." Fran looked at him expectantly.

He cleared his throat. "I suppose you know what I came here to talk to you about?"

"No, I really don't. Do you have a legal problem we can help you with?" Fran asked. "You know Tom and I are lawyers, right?"

"No, I actually didn't know that." Brent took another sip of his cola. "I've come here to ask for your daughter's hand in marriage."

Thomas laughed and took Fran's hand. "I see where the mix up is. We never actually adopted Sylvia. She isn't actually our daughter even though we think of her that way. She has a family of her own. You need to be talking to Alex Kendall."

"That's right. Jan is ours. Sweet smart little thing, you'll be glad she's Sylvia's friend."

Brent looked at the people before him. He felt sad for them. They don't realize how precious Jan is, he thought. "Mr. Dodd, I'm asking for Jan's hand in marriage. I wouldn't want to ask her without your blessing."

"See, I told you he was easy to get rid of after a couple of pitchers." Sylvia laughed as they sat down at Jan's kitchen table.

"I hate sports bars," Jan said. "Actually, that's not true. I hate going to a sports bar with a noisy jock."

"There you go. Those are my sentiments exactly." Sylvia laughed. "Too bad he's so cute. I feel a little uncomfortable." She looked at Jan. "I'm usually the one with a boyfriend."

"Syl, have you ever thought about Jeb. He's obviously smitten with you."

"Jebediah?" Sylvia sat up straight. "No, actually, I hadn't. Well, that's not entirely true. I've wondered a couple times what it would be like to kiss him but he's always been just sort of a stepping stone."

"He was a stepping stone to what?"

Sylvia looked thoughtful. "Well first he was someone to pass you off to when I took Brent." She laughed. "And we both know that's not going to happen."

"No." Jan smiled.

"Then he was just someone to ride bikes with and honestly he's been kind of a bodyguard against Vance."

"Why do you suppose he's doing all that?"

"Well." Sylvia was thoughtful. "Jan, he'll be bald in a year and he's shorter than me."

"I don't think he's shorter. I think you're the same height and I really don't think that matters very much."

"He actually has two inches on me but you're right it doesn't matter very much."

"Syl, who are the handsomest men you know?"

"Well, I hate to tell you but Brent's got to be number one."

"Yeah, and he has a lot of hair and he's really tall and he's mine." Jan laughed. "Who else do you think is handsome?"

"Well, my dad," Sylvia pondered, "and yours and there's my brother Mike." She looked at Jan. "I see what you're doing. They're all bald headed. Some of them are tall though."

"I think they're all handsome, too. I feel sorry for myself since Brent is tall and has lots of really nice hair."

"Poor thing," Sylvia said. "I hope Jeb doesn't do a comb over."

"Put your foot down. No comb over."

Sylvia stood up and picked up her purse. "I'll think about it but you know what. I don't think Jebediah wants me. There have been a couple of times when he could have kissed me but he didn't. I quit eating onions and chili. Is my breath still bad? Man-0-man, do I feel humbled."

"Your breath isn't bad. Maybe you should stay tonight. You don't have to go to work so you can wear the same clothes in the morning. You could go ahead and get the couch warmed up."

"I'm fine, Jan. I only drank one glass of beer and that was hours ago. I want to go home to my own apartment while I still have one to go to."

"I don't suppose Vance can come over there and bother you tonight since we dropped him at his house and his car is over here."

"No and if you call me in the morning, leave a message because I'm not going to answer the phone. I've got to get caller ID."

Jan's phone rang and she looked at the ID window. "It's my parents."

"I'll call you tomorrow." Sylvia waved as she went out the door.

"Hello."

"Hello, honey." It was her mother's voice.

"Is everything alright, Mom? It's almost midnight."

"Yes, but I needed to talk to you. Jan, honey, you know your father and I love you, don't you?"

"Of course, I know that, Mom. Is Dad sick or something?"

"No, we're both here and we're fine."

"I love you, too, Mom. Can I speak to Dad?" What was going on? She wouldn't be comfortable if she didn't hear his voice.

"Hello, Jan." Her father's voice was shaky. "We just wanted to be sure you knew how proud we are of you."

"Thanks, Dad, is everything alright?"

"Just fine, sweetheart, goodnight." He hung up the phone.

They must have found out she'd lost her job.

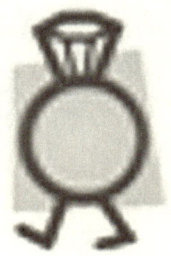

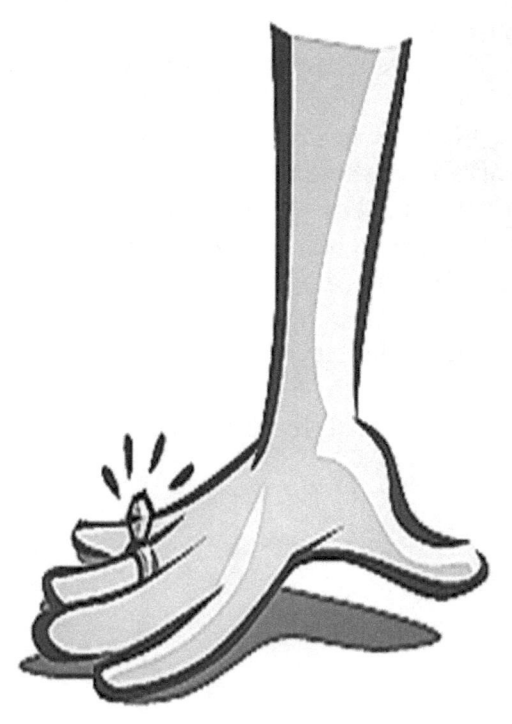

Thursday

"Why did you resign?" Brent stood at the opening to her cubicle looking fierce.

"It seems there's a policy."

"A trumped up policy." He sat down. "I just don't understand. Why would he want to get rid of you, Jan? You've saved him so much money. He's been so happy with your work."

Jan looked away as she saw the truth dawning on his face. "It's me he wants to get rid of."

She turned her back. She didn't want to see the hurt on his face.

"He gave you a choice between me and your job and you chose me." She heard the smile in his words and turned around.

"That's not exactly right, Brent. Don't give me more credit than I deserve."

"It's as close to right as I need." He turned her around in her chair and pulled her into his arms. He kissed her and she was glad he was holding her because she was sure her legs wouldn't. "It doesn't matter, Jan. I've been looking into starting my own firm. Dan gets in my way every time I try to make positive changes here. You know you and I can work together. Your parents always have." He looked at her seriously.

"Of course, we can work together but I wouldn't quit just yet, Brent." She took a deep breath and pushed away from him, testing her legs for strength. "Sylvia lost her job yesterday, too. He fired her and as mad as I am at him, I have to admit she deserved it."

"I'm paying her for decorating my house."

"Yes, but after that what will she do? You know I won't let her live on the street. Someone has to have an income."

"And you're counting on mine?"

Jan took a deep breath and looked up at him. "I was. I'm sorry. That was presumptuous."

He was smiling at her. "I'm so excited. You really trust me."

"I guess I do."

"I want you to have dinner with me tonight, okay, after we go to pet the cats. We'll make some plans then. I have something I want to show you." He kissed her again and Jan realized she was okay with all this kissing. In fact she liked it. She watched him leave her cube and smiled.

"You certainly look happy," Sylvia said to Jan as she sat down at the table. They were meeting for lunch at Brent's brother's restaurant.

"I am happy." She picked up her menu and looked it over. "I think I'll have a cheeseburger and chili fries."

"Aren't you going to pet cats with Brent this afternoon?"

"Oh yeah, I guess I'll change that." She looked at the menu again.

"I'm happy for you, JanJan." Sylvia picked up the menu and looked at it. "I hope Brent knows that I'll be a part of your lives since apparently I'm never going to find a partner."

"You'll be a big part of our lives even if you do find a partner."

"Yeah, friends for life," Sylvia said. The waitress approached and she ordered soup and salad.

Jan ordered the same thing with the dressing on the side. "So, has Vance called you today?"

"Only twice, I'm telling you Jan, the guy just doesn't give up. He wanted to go out tonight but I said no. Luckily I'm going to Brent's to take some measurements and try to get a feel for the place. You still want me to decorate, don't you? I mean I decorated your apartment."

"Of course, Syl, Brent and I have only been going out for two weeks. I'm not going to be living there for a while if ever. That is unless we both find ourselves on the street."

"Yeah, JanJan, I'm sorry I'm so much work. You swore you wouldn't take care of me anymore, remember?"

"You knew at the time I didn't mean it. Just like I know that you'll still be overprotective of me now that Brent is on the scene."

"That's right, friends for life."

"I can't believe you told John that we wanted those two kittens."

"I was going to take all three but the little one got sick. I guess it's better for John to take it if it has special needs."

"Brent." Jan slid into the booth at the restaurant where he'd brought her to dinner. "I told you I'm going to get a greyhound in a year or so. It's not a good idea to have cats, too."

"Diesel is small animal safe." Brent scooted around the half circle booth until he was sitting next to Jan. "Dee says we should use caution but she's pretty sure that he's alright with cats."

"You talked to Dee about Diesel. Did you make a commitment?"

Jan felt Brent's eyes on her but didn't look at him.

"I'm being overwhelming again." He picked up her hand. "Look at me, Jan."

She turned her head and felt her face soften when she saw his big brown eyes. She stiffened. "Will I never make another decision for myself?"

"If you don't want those cats and that dog just say so. I do get carried away sometimes but I know it. If you just tell me I'll respond."

"I'm being petty."

"You could never be petty."

"Yes, I could. The truth is that I love that dog and those kittens are adorable and you're right. I think they'll all get along."

"Good, because I think I'm already attached to them all. I hope the little one will be alright."

"John is a veterinarian. He'll take care of her," Jan said. "I guess the cats will live with me and Diesel will live with you."

"That's what I figured but not for very long I hope."

"I guess it depends on how long it takes me to get a job. I'll get another paycheck this month, so I'll be alright and Sylvia can pay her rent next month but she doesn't save anything and I don't have more than a couple of months rent in savings, maybe three."

"I was hoping you'd both come to live with me, just until Sylvia gets settled somewhere else. Then it would be just the two of us."

The waiter came and took their orders and Brent ordered a bottle of champagne.

"Brent, I don't know about living with you. I'm a very old-fashioned girl."

"I mean as my wife." Brent held out a ring box. "Will you marry me, Jan?"

Her hands went to her face and she sucked in a breath. "We've only been together for two weeks, Brent. Are you sure?"

"Completely sure, and I'm calling it a year and three months, one week and two days. That's how aware of you I've been the whole time we've worked together."

She looked up into his eyes and felt tears spring to hers. He opened the box and she looked down at the large plastic diamond ring he had won for her at the amusement park. "I wondered where that went."

"It fell off in the Ferris Wheel when you clapped your hand over your mouth."

"What a lovely memory." She smiled and put the ring on her finger. "It is too big for me."

"It's only temporary. If you say yes, we'll go and pick out an engagement ring and wedding bands together." He tipped her head up to look at him. "See, you still get to make some decisions."

She looked back down at the plastic ring.

"You're scaring me, Jan. I talked to your mom and dad last night. They gave us their blessing. Please don't say no."

"So that's why they called me last night so late." She stroked the surface of the ring with her other hand. "It probably came as a big surprise to them."

"They didn't tell you I was going to ask, did they?"

"No, they told me they loved me and were proud of me."

"Well, Jan, can you give me an answer. My palms are getting sweaty."

She smiled. "Yes, I'll marry you."

Brent put his forehead down on the table and took a deep breath. Jan stroked the back of his head and he looked up and smiled at her. The waiter approached the table with the champagne.

"You really built the suspense, JanJan. I was starting to think I'd have to send the champagne back."

Sylvia let herself into the house with the key Brent had given her. He was taking Jan out to dinner tonight. Probably to propose, she thought and was surprised by the warm feeling she got inside. She should have been wild with jealousy but all she could feel was happy for Jan.

She switched on the porch light. It was still dusk outside but it was quickly approaching dark. She turned back into the house and switched on the overhead light at the side of the door. That was one of the first things that would need to go. That overhead fan surely was one of the first ones made. She'd pick out a few samples and let Brent decide between them. It was probably better to let the customer think they had some control.

She stopped in the middle of the living room and looked at the furniture. It was clear that what Brent had said was true. It all came out of someone's basement. It had probably been stored there for years. The room even had a slightly musty smell.

After studying the large room that served as both dining room and living room she went into the kitchen. It was tiny. She could hardly turn around and there was certainly not room for two people in it. She wondered if Brent would be open to tearing down walls. Of course, that would cost more. He was going to pay her according to the amount of time spent, and supplies of course.

She jumped at the sound of the front door closing. Oh no, had Vance followed her over here. He'd turned up in all sorts of places that she didn't expect him. It was almost like he was following her. What if she was trapped in this house with him? She took a deep breath.

"Syl,"

She screamed before she realized it was Jebediah's voice that called to her then dissolved into laughter when he came through the door to the kitchen and took her arms to steady her. "What's wrong?" he demanded.

She looked into his navy blue eyes and wondered once again what it would be like to kiss him. "I guess you startled me."

He let go of her arms and said. "Well you startled me, too. That was a blood curdling scream. I thought you were being attached."

"Sorry, I'm a little jumpy these days."

"Is that Vance guy bothering you? I get a bad feeling about him."

"I think he's harmless, Jebediah, but he is bothering me a little. He shows up everywhere I go so I think he must be following me. When I heard that door shut, I immediately thought it was him." She turned and looked around the kitchen. "Do you think that Brent would be open to tearing down some walls?"

"I think it depends on what Jan thinks."

She turned around and looked at Jeb again. "Sylvia," he asked. "Are you alright with Brent and Jan being together? I know that you had your sights set for him at one point."

What a nice man, she thought.

"Thanks for your concern, Jebediah, I'm fine. I mean I figured out that Brent wasn't for me before I realized that he was after Jan. I just thought that would be the end of it. I didn't think he'd continue after Jan."

"I know you didn't. I knew he would, though. She's the first woman he's ever seemed to care about. He's dated a little but he never just went after someone like that before."

Sylvia wrote a few notes on the clip board she was carrying. "This room is just too small."

"I told him that when he bought the house six months ago but he said he was the only one who was ever in it."

"I guess Jan will be spending time in it with him, now, if he asks her to marry him. She's a very old-fashioned girl."

"He'll ask her; in fact, I suspect that's what he's doing now."

"So you didn't come here to see Brent?"

"No, I talked to Brent earlier and he told me he'd given you his key. He said he was taking Jan to dinner so I put two and two together and figured he was going to ask her to marry him and you were coming to work on the interior design of his house."

"Deductive thinking,"

"I'm sorry you lost your job, Syl." He followed her back into the living room.

She was looking at the dining area which was on the other side of the wall that she wanted to remove in the kitchen. "I'm used to being fired. It's still traumatic, though. Like I told Jan, this whole thing has been a humbling experience."

"What else has humbled you?"

"Oh, discovering that what you look like just isn't that important."

"You mean because Brent chose Jan instead of you. You know Jan isn't a knockout like you are but she's very attractive."

"Jan's beautiful. She just doesn't want anyone to know it. She's always been that way. It was like we played this little game with each other. I was the knockout and she was the plain Jan."

"Well, I wouldn't let Brent's feelings for her bother you about your looks. He's oblivious to that kind of stuff."

"Well, there is also the fact that even though Brent is incredibly handsome, I wasn't really interested in him either."

"So why are you humbled?"

"Well, I don't know how to look at myself as anything but an attractive woman. I mean, should I stop trying, Jebediah?"

"What do you mean stop trying?" Jeb sat down on the wooden bench that Brent and Jan had occupied the week before and pulled Sylvia down next to him.

"I mean am I too vain. Should I stop styling my hair in an attractive way? Should I stop dressing the way I do?"

Jeb took her hand and squeezed it. Sylvia felt her heart thump.

"Syl, you know I specialize in geriatrics, don't you?"

"Yes, Jan told me, why?"

"One of the most difficult problems we deal with when people get older is the loss of their beauty. Even the most beautiful people fade when they get older. It's one of the major causes of depression that I see in my practice."

"You're not making me feel better."

"Give me a minute." He squeezed her hand again. "The saddest thing is when I see a woman or a man who was beautiful in youth and in the effort to maintain that beauty they had all sorts of surgery, but at a point the surgery doesn't work anymore. In fact they just end up looking weird."

"Like I said, Jebediah, you're not making me feel better."

"All I'm trying to say is it isn't healthy to be too concerned with what you look like. The beauty inside of you never fades unless you haven't nurtured it."

"What a beautiful thing to say, Jebediah." She looked down at their joined hands. "So does that mean that I should stop enhancing my beauty, maybe cut my hair, stop wearing miniskirts?"

"No, there's nothing wrong with looking your best. When I get up in the morning, I take a shower and comb what little hair I have left." He smiled and Sylvia blushed.

She put her hand to her face. She rarely blushed.

"I always dress in polo shirts." Jeb continued. "They look nice on me and I never wear colors that make me look washed out. I look well-groomed."

"Yes you always look well-groomed." She looked into his eyes. "And I like the way certain colors make your eyes change shades of blue."

"I'm glad you've noticed." He smiled. "My point is that you can't help it if being well-groomed and looking your best means being drop dead gorgeous."

"You're making me feel better now." They were looking at each other eye to eye and she leaned toward him.

The front door burst open and Vance stormed halfway across the room and put his hands on his hips. "Look, Jebediah Webb," he said. "I've about had it with you trying to move in on my girlfriend."

"Vance, what are you doing here?" Sylvia said as she and Jeb stood and faced him. "You really are following me, aren't you?"

"I have a right. This isn't the first time I've caught the two of you together and when I looked in that window he was about to kiss you."

"Look, Vance," Sylvia said. "I am not your girlfriend."

"I'm getting ready to take you out of the picture, old man." Vance turned away from Sylvia and moved toward Jeb.

"Vance, don't. We've all had about enough of this." Jeb put up a hand in a gesture for Vance to stop. He did. "I believe the lady has told you that she doesn't want to see you anymore." Jeb spoke quietly but firmly.

Vance looked back at Sylvia. "You didn't ever mean that did you, sugar? You were just teasing me."

"Were you teasing him, Sylvia?" Jeb looked at her.

"No."

"You kept going out with me. Why did you do that?" Vance whined

"Well, because you insisted and we've only been out alone one time."

"Come on, sugar." Vance turned back to Sylvia. "We got chemistry. We been saying that all along."

"You've been saying it."

"Vance," Jeb interrupted. "Never mind the fact that the lady is old enough to be your mother's younger sister." He smiled sideways at her. "I don't think you have that much in common."

"We got chemistry." Vance moved in Jeb's direction again.

"That's enough, Vance, leave the lady alone and go home." Jeb stood straight and his voice was commanding.

"Who's going to make me?" Vance stormed in Jeb's direction.

"I am." Jeb stood his ground

Sylvia sucked in her breath and moved to get in between the burly youth and Jebediah.

But Vance stopped and looked back at her. "Well, if you feel that way about it." He said looking pouty. "How old are you, anyway?"

"I've told you, Vance, I'm thirty five."

"I don't remember you telling me that." He turned and went to the door. He stopped and turned around. "Oh Sylvia, I almost forgot. Your bike came in today. We'll have it all cleaned up for you by noon tomorrow." He turned and closed the door behind him.

Sylvia looked at Jebediah.

"Don't give me a hard time about the age comment," he said.

"That was exciting. You're exciting."

Jeb took a deep breath. "Listen Sylvia, I feel very strongly about you. In fact, I'm pretty sure I'm in love with you."

She smiled at him and put down her clipboard. "Jebediah, ever since that first night we went out I've wondered what it would be like to kiss someone my own height."

"I've got two inches on you."

"Same thing, there have been lots of times when you could have kissed me but you didn't."

"You didn't kiss me either."

"That's true, will you now? I promise I'll kiss you back."

"Come over here." He pulled her to the stairway that led to the second floor. "You stand on the first step." He stepped to the one above her and turned her around. "This is what it feels like to kiss me when I'm taller than you." He lowered his lips to hers then stepped to the one below her. "And this is what it's like to kiss me when I'm shorter than you." He looked up at her and pulled her lips to his. Then he stepped to the stair she stood on. "And this is what it's like to kiss me eye to eye." Their lips touched and Sylvia forgot what she was doing.

Saturday

"So where are we going?" Jan asked Sylvia when they'd gotten into her car. It was 9 am and she would ordinarily be running but Sylvia had insisted she run an errand with her.

"We're going to the bike shop."

"I thought you picked up your bike yesterday. You know you should have sent it back, now that we're unemployed."

"Jebediah paid for it. We're going to pick out a bike for you."

"I can't afford a bike, Syl. I still have rent to pay and no income to pay it with."

"Jebediah's going to pay for the bike. I think he's pretty well-off."

"He can't buy me a bike. That's not right." Jan could see that she was going to lose that argument so she changed it. "Besides, I don't want a bike. I'm sorry, Sylvia. I'm glad you've found this sport that you love so much but I'm afraid I can't share it with you. I'm still sore from the ride we took two weeks ago."

"That's just because you're riding the wrong bike."

"There's another reason not to buy me a bike. I already have a bike." Jan had seen that determined look on Sylvia's face before. She was probably going to go home with a new bike today.

"Aren't you listening, JanJan? You've been riding the wrong bike."

"That's what Jeb said."

"When did he talk to you about it?"

"When we ran together last Sunday, or maybe it was the Sunday before. Time is kind of running all together these days."

"I know. It's great the way all of a sudden things change." Sylvia smiled

"So which one did you like the best?" Jan asked.

"Which what did I like the best?"

"Which kiss?"

"Oh they were all spectacular. I don't think I've ever been kissed like that."

"You're blushing." Jan laughed. "Syl, you never blush. You must have really fallen for this guy."

"I have, I think I had all along but I wasn't paying attention to my feelings for him. I was all caught up in trying to get Brent's attention and then I was worried about you. I forgot to pay attention to my own feelings."

"That's a switch."

"Yeah," Sylvia smiled. "Anyway, I don't know what's going to happen next. He didn't ask me to marry him or anything."

"Are you ready for that? If he asks will you say yes?"

"I'm pretty sure I will. I really love him, JanJan. Here we are." She pulled into the parking lot and they got out of the car. "Jebediah says we should look at comfort bikes. Brent doesn't like to ride bending over either so he uses a mountain bike but Jeb says that with your flat ass and big hips you'll do better on a comfort bike."

"Oh great, I'm glad my flat ass and big hips are a subject of conversation."

"He didn't actually say that. That was my translation. He said with your compact body type you would do better on a comfort bike." Sylvia smiled. "He's so smart. Who'd have ever thought I'd find brains so sexy."

They loaded the shiny blue comfort bike onto the bike rack on the back of Sylvia's car and got in. The car didn't start the first time and Sylvia pumped the gas pedal and tried again. It started up noisily and a puff of dark smoke could be seen rising from the back of the car.

"How old is this car now?" Jan asked.

"Well, considering it was old when I got it and I've had it for five years, it's really old now."

"I hope it lasts a little longer. We can't afford a new one anytime soon."

"Poor JanJan, you're always so worried about money. I can't believe you insisted on buying that bike. Jeb wanted to buy one for you. It was his idea. He really likes you and he was just sure you'd enjoy riding with us if you have the right bike."

"I can't just let him buy me a bike."

"What about Brent? Now that you're going to marry him would you let him support you?"

"No, we'll support each other. I'll never stop working. I like to work."

"You like that job that you do at Baxter?"

Jan smiled sadly. "You mean that job I used to do. Believe it or not I do like it. Brent likes what he does, too."

"I know. I think that's why I found him so boring."

"You find me boring, too, don't you?"

"Yes but you're very pliable. I can always get you to do something exciting with me if I need to. That's what started this whole thing remember?"

"That's true. Sylvia," Jan said. "Do you have any plans? I mean what are we going to do about the jobless thing."

"No, I don't have any plans. I don't want to think about it right now."

"We have to think about it sometime. You can't just keep letting other people take care of you. Don't you want to do something valuable in the world?"

"I'm doing the interior decorating thing."

"Do you plan to pursue it? I mean Brent will let you do whatever you want at his house and you said Jeb's house was almost empty so you've probably got another job. But you'll have to market yourself to make a go of it."

"Oh, JanJan, it sounds so businesslike. I can't market myself. I wouldn't know where to start." Sylvia pulled the car into the space at Jan's apartment building. She looked straight ahead sadly. "Can't I just be happy for a little while without having to think about what a failure I am?"

"I'm sorry, Syl. I didn't mean to drag you down," Jan said as she followed Sylvia out of the car and they worked together to take the bike off of the rack and pushed it to her apartment. She unlocked the door. "Sylvia, don't be mad. You're right, I'm too intense."

"I'm not mad," Sylvia said but she sounded sad. "You were probably just getting me back for that comment about your flat ass and big hips. You know, JanJan, I really think you have a nice figure. You're compact but shapely."

"Thanks Syl, but you still seem sad."

"No, I'm not sad. Now remember to put next Sunday aside to ride with us. Jebediah and Brent and Ben always ride together once a month. They get together and decide which

Sunday will be the best for all three. Then they give up their volunteer work or whatever they might have had planned and they go for that ride. It keeps their friendship together. Isn't that nice?"

"Yeah," Jan smiled. "And we're going to be part of that now. That is nice. Do you want to get some lunch before we go to the greyhound rescue?"

"No thanks, I don't think I'll go to the rescue today. Sorry, Jan. I'll see you tomorrow at Mass."

"Sylvia, come on, cheer up."

"I'm fine," she said and left.

Jan wanted to kick herself. Hadn't she learned by now? This was the whole problem. She was always trying to mold Sylvia into someone she just couldn't be. Maybe she'd talk to Brent about it.

Sylvia pulled her car into Jeb's driveway and turned the key. The car trembled for a minute then backfired. Sylvia didn't even notice it anymore. She got out of the car and started up the walk toward the house. The door opened and Jeb rushed out.

"What happened?" Jeb hurried up to her and took her arm. "Are you alright? What was that huge bang?"

She looked at his handsome face and wondered why she'd never noticed how beautiful he was. "That was my car." She laughed. "It always does that when I turn it off."

"Oh Sylvia, I didn't know this old thing was yours," Jeb said looking at the ancient automobile. "I've seen it in the parking lot at your apartment but we always took my car. You poor thing, how long have you been driving this car."

"Five years, it was Jan's before that. Her parents bought it for her when she left home. It took her until she was thirty to save enough money to get a new car. The car my parents gave me died about the same time and well, I have no credit and I didn't have a job at the time. I'm lucky to have it." She felt her shoulders drop and took a deep breath.

"Well, I get the feeling your luck is about to run out on this car."

"Oh, I don't know, it's been doing that for a couple of years now but it keeps on going."

"So what's up, Syl. Come on in." He propelled her toward the house. "I'm thrilled that you're here so early but I won't have dinner ready for hours."

"I know. I just wanted to see you."

"Good." He opened the door for her and she stepped into the empty living room. Sylvia stopped and looked around.

It had so much potential. The high ceiling with the long flat wall, she'd love to arrange that whole wall with artwork, her own and the works of her favorite artists.

"You'll decorate it won't you?" Jeb said from behind her. She turned and looked at him and her face must have given away her distress because he stepped forward and took her arms. "What's the matter, Sylvia?"

To her horror she started to cry. Jeb put his arms around her and she put her head on his shoulder. He felt big and strong and comforting. Had his shoulders always been so broad?

"What is it, sweetheart?"

"You said you loved me. Do you still feel that way?"

"Very much." He pushed her slightly away to look at her and she scrubbed at her eyes. "You said you felt the same way about me. Have you changed your mind?"

Sylvia looked into his eyes and she could see the love and the concern. "No, it seems like things are going really fast but I'm still all fluttery when you touch me."

"Good." He kissed her lightly on the mouth. "Come into the kitchen and tell me what's bothering you." He guided her through the empty house to the warm comfortable kitchen. "I was just pouring myself some lemonade."

She sat down at the counter and he poured two glasses of lemonade, put them down then sat on a stool across from her. "What made you cry? Something tells me you don't cry easily."

"I don't cry easy but it always feels like a relief when I do. I feel better now."

"Good, do you want to tell me about it or is there another reason for your visit?"

"I guess you know I got fired from Baxter and Company."

"Yeah, you told me. That's why I paid for the bike, remember? You were going to send it back and I didn't want you to because we ride together."

"That's right. Wasn't it funny how Vance greeted us like good friends when we went to pick it up on Friday?"

"Yeah, I don't know if he was acting or if he was sincerely happy to see us."

"I don't think he's capable of that kind of acting. Anyway, did you know that Jan lost her job, too?"

"You're kidding. I thought she was Daniel Baxter's pride and joy."

"She was, but it seems that there was a policy against her dating Brent. Well, I mean against romantic involvement between employees."

"Oh, poor Jan, she really likes that job."

"Yeah, well, anyway we went to get her a bike today and you know how you showed me the bikes in the shop that would work for her."

"Yes, and did she find one."

"She did. I just dropped it and her off. She insisted on paying for it herself. She wouldn't let me call you for your credit card number like you told me to."

"I'm not surprised. Jan strikes me as the type to insist on paying her way. Maybe you should have taken me along. I feel bad now. I didn't realize she was out of a job."

"Well, she'll be working out her two week notice. So she has another paycheck coming. And JanJan always has tons of money in savings. I figured now that she's engaged to Brent, she wouldn't have to save anymore because she'll move into his house and she won't have to pay rent or put a down payment on a house."

"So, am I missing something? Why did Jan buying a bike make you cry?"

"Well." She sipped her lemonade. "Well, she was just so worried about money and..." She looked across the table at Jeb. "Jebediah, I can't hold a job. I'm a terrible failure. Jan has taken care of me all my life."

"You are not a failure. Don't say that about yourself. You didn't belong in that job. You probably didn't belong in any of the jobs you've had."

"But, Jebediah, everyone has to make a living and I've never been able to."

"You're starting your interior decorating and when you've finished that you'll decorate my house. You're on your way."

"Jan said I would need to market myself. There is no way that's going to happen. I wouldn't know where to start. Then I got thinking and even if I could make a living at it, I can't do the business end. I mean I'm sure there is bookkeeping and there would be a lot of legal stuff and I just can't do it."

"Well, you don't have to. You can hire someone to do that stuff for you."

"My point here, Jebediah, is that you need to know these awful things about me before you get really involved."

He smiled at her and reached across the bar to take her hand. "Too late, I'm already really involved. I don't believe you're a failure. Your artwork is spectacular and I can't wait to go to your parents' farm and see the rest of it."

"Yeah, but it's just art. It isn't anything valuable to the world."

"That's not true. Art is very important to the world." He stood and pulled her into the living room. "I want you to decorate this whole house and I want you to do it exactly like your apartment."

"But that's not right. I have to get a feeling for what you want. It's your house."

"I was hoping you'd share it with me. I want you to come and live here with me."

She was silent.

"You'll need a place to go and like you said, you don't want to live with Jan and Brent."

She looked at the high ceiling and then sadly at Jeb. "I'm sorry, Jebediah, but I'm as old-fashioned as Jan is."

"That was a really clumsy way for me to ask you to marry me. I'm sorry. I guess you need to know that I'm kind of a social klutz."

"You were asking me to marry you?"

"Yes." He took both of her hands. "Listen, Sylvia, I want you to say you'll marry me and I want to sweep you up and run straight downtown to city hall and get it done before you change your mind. But I think, like you said before, that's moving a little fast. Not that I am ever going to change the way I feel about you."

"So you're not asking me to marry you."

"Yes, I am but not right away. I want you to wear my ring but I want you to be my fiancé for a little while before the wedding. I want us to go through all the right steps. I want us to get married in the church and go to the premarital classes that they insist on, all of that. But if your need for a place to live comes up before the wedding, I don't see any reason why you shouldn't move in with me. You know in biblical days all a man had to do to marry a woman was to move her into his house and call her his wife."

"Really?"

"According to the historians," he said.

"Jebediah, you know I probably won't be able to contribute to the income. When I asked Jan if she would let Brent support her she said, "We'll support each other." She said she would always work. How can you and I support each other if I can't contribute?"

"There are a lot of kinds of support. You'll contribute in your own way. Listen, I make a pretty good living. There is no reason why we'll need any more money than I make. I'm not filthy rich but judging by the car you're driving, you're used to stretching your dollars."

"But it would be your money. I'd never really have money of my own."

"It will all be your own. When we're married we'll be a family. It's family money. It says in the bible when a man marries a woman they are "Same Flesh". We'll be like one person with two different personalities."

"Jan says I should do something valuable."

"I'm sure Jan will agree with me that making our home a beautiful place to live and producing art that beautifies the world is valuable. Not to mention making me the happiest man with the most beautiful wife in the kingdom."

Sylvia laughed. "You said you were with the most beautiful woman in the kingdom the night we went to Medieval Times."

"I was already in love with you then."

"And I acted like such an ass."

"No you didn't. You just had your mind set in a different direction."

"What about the vanity thing. You know I do know what I look like."

"It doesn't matter what you look like. I just want you to keep that in mind. Besides that ..." He took her in his arms and kissed her until she was dizzy. "I think I can stand having the most beautiful woman in the kingdom for my wife."

Sylvia felt disoriented as he looked at her, still holding her close. "You haven't answered me yet Sylvia, will you marry me?"

"Uh huh..."

"Make that a word."

"Yes, Jebediah, I love you." He kissed her again and she didn't care what she was doing.

"Hey, darlin, ready to get some dinner?" Brent said when Jan opened the door of her apartment. He came in and she put her arms around his neck and kissed him.

"Hmmm ... what a nice greeting," he said putting his arms around her waist and kissing her back.

"I couldn't wait to see you. I thought about you all afternoon while I was working on the dogs. It's fun to be in love."

"It is fun. I'm glad you were thinking about me."

"Well, when I wasn't worrying about Sylvia I was thinking about you."

"What's wrong with Sylvia?"

"I hurt her feelings today."

"Whose bike is this?" Brent was looking at the new blue comfort bike standing propped on the wall behind the door.

"It's mine. Sylvia insisted on me getting it today. See what I mean. We can't afford to be spending money on a new bike right now. We have rent to pay."

"Did she buy the bike?" Brent studied it. He picked up the back of the bike and spun the wheel. Then put it down and sat on it. "It's a great bike. I've thought about one of these for myself."

"She didn't buy it. I did."

He looked at her and smiled. "Why did you buy yourself a new bike if you can't afford it?"

"Sylvia made me."

"Oh, darlin, you're a trip." Brent leaned the bike back up against the wall and put his arm across Jan's shoulders. "Let's go into the kitchen and get a beer. You can tell me about it while you shower and change for dinner. Judging by the smell you just got back from the rescue."

"How can I tell you about it from the shower?"

"I'll sit on the toilet." Brent laughed at her horrified look. "With the seat down and my pants up."

"No, Brent. I'm not ready for that yet. I have a clear shower curtain."

Brent grinned broader and opened the refrigerator. He opened a beer and offered it to her. "I guess you'll have to tell me about it before you take your shower." He sat down at the table and she sat across from him.

"Do I stink?"

"You smell like dogs. That's a nice smell but they might not let us into the restaurant. Now tell me, why are you worried about Sylvia? What did you do to hurt her feelings?"

"I was asking her what she was going to do next. I mean about finding a job. She accused me of always worrying about money. But Brent, how can I help worrying about money when I always have to support her. I love her dearly but she doesn't even try."

"Oh, I think you're wrong about that, Jan. I'll never forget when she first started at the firm. She tried so hard. She even wore these boring suits all the time. Like the ones you wear." Brent stopped and looked at Jan.

He sucked in his breath and leaned back in his chair. Her eyes seemed to bore holes in him but she didn't say anything. "Your suits look wonderful on you but on her with all that long blond hair and long lean figure. It just looked silly."

"So you've noticed that she's beautiful."

"Of course I have. How could anyone not notice that?" He looked at her warily. "Anyway, she came in looking all businesslike and Jennifer, the supervisor of that group, started to train her. Jennifer came to me after about a week feeling frustrated. She said that Sylvia obviously really wanted to do that job but she just didn't have the attention span for it. She said she caught on fast but tended to forget what she was doing."

Jan looked at her hands folded together on the table in front of her. "She wanted to do it for me."

"That's what I figured. She really wanted to be successful so that you could stop worrying about her. She really wanted to take care of herself."

"I asked her today if she didn't want to do something valuable to the world. What a mean thing to say."

"Don't beat up on yourself too much, darlin. You're in kind of a tough position. I wish you'd relax and let me help you with it." He put his large hand on her small crossed ones. "You know, you don't have to save the world alone. We're together in this now."

Jan looked down at their joined hands. She didn't dare look at his face. She might cry and she really didn't want to. "What is the answer then Brent? I've spent the last fifteen years stuffing her into jobs that she can't do but I don't have access to the ones that she can do. I don't even know what they are?"

"I have an idea."

The phone rang and Jan looked at the caller ID. Webb, Jebediah, MD, it read. "It's Jeb."

"Answer it."

"Hello."

"JanJan." It was Sylvia.

"Yes, I was expecting Jeb. The caller ID had his name."

"I'm at his house. We've had the most delightful afternoon. We went to the farmers market and bought all sorts of great things to cook for dinner tonight. Jebediah is going to teach me how to use his attention deficit disorder kitchen. Did you know he works with ADD seniors? He says it's a big problem in the geriatric community. Can you believe this problem is not just for kids and adults, but for seniors, too?"

"No, I didn't know that."

"Jebediah says I have to stop calling it a deficiency. It's just a different style of living. Anyway..." Jan could hear the excitement in Sylvia's voice. "We're going to cook an ADD gourmet meal and we want you and Brent to eat it with us."

"They want us to join them for dinner," Jan said to Brent.

"Sounds great but you have to take a shower first." Brent stood and left the room.

"He says I smell like dogs," Jan said to Sylvia. "We'd love to come. Let me shower and change and we'll be right there."

"Jan, I hope I didn't insult you when I made that comment about your pants suits."

"Brent." Jan gasped and tried to cover herself with her hands. The water of the shower was steamy and that helped. "I told you I wasn't ready for this."

He sat on the closed lid of the toilet across the room from the shower. "Don't worry, that shower curtain isn't really clear. It's kind of cloudy. So did I insult you?"

Jan relaxed very gradually and continued to lather herself up in the steamy water. "You surprised me. I didn't realize that you'd noticed how beautiful Sylvia is and I don't really understand why you chose me if you did."

"I didn't choose you. That was love at first sight. Well, I guess you could say that it was love at first sight that grew with every encounter I had with you. By the time Sylvia came along I was a lost cause. I would never have been interested in her anyway. She's just not my type."

"Hmmm..." Jan turned off the shower. "Now leave while I get out. I'm really not ready for that yet."

"Okay."

They arrived at Jeb's house an hour later. Brent opened the door and called out. "We're here so if you're making out, quit now."

"We're in the kitchen," Sylvia called back.

They walked through the empty house into the bright kitchen. "I guess you'll be decorating this house next," Brent said.

"After I finish yours," Sylvia was glowing.

"You look like you're feeling better. You looked pretty sad when you left my house this afternoon." Jan sat on a stool at the counter. "I'm sorry if I insulted you, Syl."

"It's not your fault I'm a failure."

"Don't say that about yourself," Jeb and Jan said together.

"Well, I'm too happy to be upset now anyway." Sylvia held up her left hand to display a diamond ring set in a white gold band.

"Sylvia!" Jan jumped down from her stool and ran around the counter to embrace her friend. "You and Jeb?"

Sylvia nodded. "He asked me this afternoon and I said yes."

"Congratulations, Jeb." Brent shook Jeb's hand over the counter. "I guess we'll be getting married at the same time. How did you get a ring so fast? We ordered Jan's ring, but it won't be in until next week."

"I liked this one and they had it on display. I don't think I could wait a week," Sylvia said. "JanJan." She looked at her friend. "You won't have to take care of me anymore. Jebediah says I don't even have to work if I don't want to. We went through the whole house trying to decide which room to make into my studio. I decided on the attic. The light is perfect."

"Your own studio, Syl, and it isn't in a barn loft. That's great. I can still take care of you a little, can't I? Old habits are hard to break," Jan said.

"That's my idea," Brent said. "I was thinking that Jan could do your books for you. I don't think all of her time will be taken up on our company. So if you want to do some interior decorating on the side she could help you. Couldn't you, Jan? You're really good at keeping accounts. And my degree is in marketing. I could spare a little time to help out there."

"Our company?" Jan said.

"Yes, I talked to your parents about drawing up the legal papers for me, after I asked for your hand in marriage." Brent smiled. "They thought I was confused. They thought I was asking for Sylvia."

"So that's why they called me that night to tell me they love me. They felt guilty."

"I think they did." Brent laughed. "Then we talked about my company."

"You've been talking about starting up your own firm for a while," Jeb said as he poured glasses of wine all around.

"Yeah, and the really funny thing is that I've talked some of Dan's stockholders into backing me as well. I'm going to begin a training program. I'm thinking of a program to provide insurance adjusters for insurance companies all over the world. I love to teach and that's the area where Dan always got in my way. It's very important for us to remember that we're dealing with people under disaster conditions. We have to be compassionate."

"And I'm going to do the books?" Jan asked.

"I was hoping you would. We can work together, darlin. Your parents do and they seem to have a great marriage."

"Yeah, they do," Sylvia said. "And you think JanJan will have time to do my books, too?"

"At least at first," Brent said. "If our businesses take off we'll hire someone else.

Labor Day the following year

"This scrap book is beautiful, Sylvia." Jan flipped the pages of the book that lay on the picnic table. They were in Jeb and Sylvia's backyard for a picnic.

"Look, Brent, she starts with Medieval Times. You and I were such hams that night." Jan pointed to a picture of her on the horse with a gown of pale blue draped over the horse's side. Brent stood at the head of the horse dressed in armor and holding a sword.

"Look at us." Sylvia pointed to the picture of Jeb on the horse with a gown draped over the side. She held the sword. "Talk about hams."

Brent sat at the table next to Jan. He ran his hand over her rounded belly. "That was one year ago, remember. We worked pretty fast getting our family started."

"My biological clock is ticking. We couldn't afford to waste time." Jan put her hand over his just in time to feel the baby kick. They both laughed and Jan blushed.

"How are you feeling, Sylvia?" Brent asked. "Have you stopped throwing up?"

"She never really did throw up much." Jeb wiped the sweat off his brow. He and Ben had been playing volleyball. Jan's parents were sitting with Brent's brother and his wife and his mother across the lawn.

"Typical of me, I threw up on into the fifth month." Jan laughed.

"That's right," Brent said. "I felt so bad for you." He squeezed her shoulder. "And now she says we'll have another one as soon as the doctor gives the go ahead."

"I was an only child, Brent. I don't want my kids to grow up alone."

"You weren't alone, JanJan," Sylvia said. "You had me."

"That's true. I think I heard a car pull in, Sylvia, maybe it's your family."

"It takes more than one car to bring my family." She rubbed her hand over her still flat belly. "We're having an only child. Mamma, Daddy, Barb!" She rushed off to greet her family as a second car load pulled into the driveway.

"So are you as excited to be an expecting Dad as I am?" Brent asked Jeb.

"I am. I hope our kids get along. Wouldn't it be great if they were as close as we are?"

"Well," Ben said. "My kids will be babysitters for yours, I guess."

"Yeah, that's nice. You won't have to do it. You can just send your kids." They looked at the yard where Ben and Shannon's children were playing croquet. Sylvia's older nieces and nephews joined them and Sylvia came back across the lawn carrying the toddler on her hip, her sister Barbara right behind her.

"This is little Punjab." She kissed the toddler's cheek and smiled at Jan, Brent, and Jeb.

"His name is Christopher," her sister said.

"I'll always think of him as Punjab, Barb. It's just love." Sylvia looked at Jeb and grinned. She looked at Jan and Brent and said. "Next year we'll have a swimming pool. Did I show you my plan?"

"You did," Jan said. "It was so beautiful I wanted to frame it and hang it on my wall."

"She's done a great job with this place." Jeb kissed Sylvia and smiled at Brent. "Your place doesn't look bad either."

"Her designs for the office are excellent."

"Thanks guys, you can stop now. I guess I'm not a failure after all." Sylvia set the toddler on the grass and walked behind him as he explored the yard. "But I'm stopping for a while. I'm going to concentrate on raising our child."

"Oh look, Brent." Jan pointed to a picture in the scrap book. It was of her at the amusement park. Brent was holding her hand and placing the large plastic diamond ring on it. She and Brent were looking into each other's eyes. "I loved you then and I didn't even know it, and I love that plastic diamond."

"Let's make this a tradition," Jeb said, "Labor Day at our house."

"Memorial Day at ours," Jan smiled at her friends and family then jumped as the baby gave her another swift kick. "I think this kid is going to play soccer." She looked across the yard at the two greyhounds playing tug with each other and sighed contentedly. Sylvia had adopted one shortly after she and Brent had brought home Diesel.

"I'm glad they get along," Sylvia said. "And I'm glad we're friends forever, Jan."

"I'm glad, too; Syl. I'm glad, too."